SARAH HAMMOND

OXFORD
UNIVERSITY PRESS

OXFORD
UNIVERSITY PRESS

Great Clarendon Street, Oxford OX2 6DP

Oxford University Press is a department of the University of Oxford.
It furthers the University's objective of excellence in research, scholarship,
and education by publishing worldwide in

Oxford   New York

Auckland   Cape Town   Dar es Salaam   Hong Kong   Karachi
Kuala Lumpur   Madrid   Melbourne   Mexico City   Nairobi
New Delhi   Shanghai   Taipei   Toronto

With offices in

Argentina   Austria   Brazil   Chile   Czech Republic   France   Greece
Guatemala   Hungary   Italy   Japan   Poland   Portugal   Singapore
South Korea   Switzerland   Thailand   Turkey   Ukraine   Vietnam

Oxford is a registered trade mark of Oxford University Press
in the UK and in certain other countries

British Library Cataloguing in Publication Data

Data available

ISBN: 978-0-19-273319-1

3 5 7 9 10 8 6 4 2

Printed in Great Britain
Paper used in the production of this book is a natural,
recyclable product made from wood grown in sustainable forests
The manufacturing process conforms to the environmental
regulations of the country of origin

For my parents and for Shawn

Prologue

I'm going to sit very quietly and wait: that's what you do with animals so they're not scared of you. The mother-dog is watching me from her bed at the other end of the living-room. I'm miles away from her babies but she's still worried.

'Are you all right in there, Mikey?'

It's the dog-lady. She's in the kitchen with Mum. They're worried too because I came out of hospital today.

'Yes!' I shout back quick so they don't come in and check on me.

It hurts behind my eyes when I speak. Little stars everywhere. I put my hands up to my head but then I stop—I don't want to touch the skin because of all the stitches down the back.

Mother-dog whines. I hold my breath. The puppies are waking up.

A little black nose sticks up out of the basket. Little paws. A black puppy rolls down onto the carpet. My legs are so whizzy I want to run about but I stay still. Pup's legs are wobbly—he can't walk straight. Falls over. Wags his tail. Stands up again. I don't move. He snuffles the edge of the blue rug.

Here's the next one! Bigger. Fatter. A bit brown and a bit black. Jumps on the black one. They roll over and over. Paws and ears and open pink mouths. I'm fizzing all over but I stay still, I stay still.

Mother-dog shuffles around. She's got more room in bed now. The dog-lady said there were three, so where's the other one?

The big one has got a ruler in his mouth. He's chuffed to bits, trotting round the chair with it. King of the Ruler. He goes stumbly when he gets to the newspapers on the floor and drops it. He cries and scratches the carpet. He can't pick it up again.

I lean forwards to help him. Mother-dog gets up, growls. Uh-oh. I sit back down quick. My neck cricks. Lightning shoots up my head and I scrunch up on the floor. The carpet smells of dog. My ears are under water. My scar aches. My head is black black black.

Breathe slowly, Mikey. In and out, in . . . and . . . out . . .

There's something wet on my cheek. I open one eye. A little furry face. He licks me again and sits down on the carpet. I open the other eye. It's the last puppy. He's all brown except for one black ear. He's watching me with his head on one side. His baby-ears flop over, can't stand up properly yet.

Mother-dog growls again. I don't move. The puppy snuggles up against my shoulder. Warm and cosy. The black in my head is going. He's guarding me—the dog-lady said there was a bit of German Shepherd in them, like real guard dogs. His fur tickles my cheek. I still don't move but I can't stop my mouth from smiling.

I've found him. This is the one I'll choose.

This is my puppy.

He can come home to look after us now that Dad has gone.

Chapter One

Timmer and me have been locked out again and I've forgotten my key, so we're going to spend the night in the shed. I bet Mum thinks I'm already in bed but I'm not—we went for an extra-long walk because Timmer is four today. He wags his tail. He likes it in the shed better than in the house. I do too. It's quiet and safe in there. I don't have to listen to lots of noises jab jab jabbing in my head.

The moon is a bright white eye in the sky tonight. It makes the night-garden different to the day-garden. There is scuffling in the shadows. Things are hiding in the dark. The leaves on the apple tree are silver and they whisper secrets to each other when the wind blows. I shiver, even though it's warm, because I know about secret things.

Timmer barks once and walks down the garden, wagging his tail. He wants to go to the shed but I have to check on Mum first.

The windows are like silent TVs in the dark. I stand and watch. I can see Mum at the kitchen table. There's make-up down her face so she's got long black tears down her cheeks. She's drinking beer out of a bottle. She's got the photos out again and she's wobbling. I hate it when she's like this.

I take a step closer and put my hands on the glass.

Mum doesn't notice me. I should be able to help her but I can't. Even if I was sitting next to her and tried to hug her, I couldn't. I've tried lots of times. She would still be far away.

I can hear the noises in the shadows behind me getting louder. The shadows always get louder when Mum's like this. The doctor said not to be upset and remember they are just my worries but I don't like it when they come to life. I ignore them and stare at Mum. She puts her head in her hands. Her shoulders shake. Timmer rubs against my leg. He's waiting. I stand for a minute longer. I can't go quite yet, Timmer: not till I'm sure she's getting better again.

The warm wind blows my hair around. Doesn't make me cool though—it's still hot. I hear Gavin'n'Tina clinking glasses and plates next-door because they're eating outside. Albert lives on the other side but he'll be in bed—he always stays inside when it gets dark. I've made a misty circle on the window. I can't see Mum properly now. I wipe it quick.

Mum stands up. She's facing the other way but she smooths down her hair and pours herself a glass of water. I smile and rub behind Timmer's ears. It's OK now, Timmer-dog. Let's go. We'll still be able to hear her from the shed if she needs us.

It's my space, the shed. I've made a chair on the floor out of the squishy bits inside the sun-lounger. It smells of suntan lotion. I pull it into the corner, opposite the door, and sit down. I'm squashed between the lawnmower and the workbench. If anyone looks in the window, they can't see me. I'm hidden.

Ahhhhhhhh, this is the business! Quiet, quiet, quiet. Moonlight shines through the little window. Timmer turns in circles and then curls up right next to me. It's hot with him so close but I don't mind—he keeps me safe.

I can feel the Backwards pulling at me but I'm not quite ready yet.

I lean back. Timmer has his nose on my knee. The lawnmower fuel smell makes my head go woolly. I like it. It all swims.

The world is going swirly; the Backwards is coming and it is bringing secrets with it. I stroke Timmer's head and rub along his spine just the way he likes it. I make his scruffy fur even messier. What will we see today, Timmer-dog? What's been happening in my shed?

The Backwards is my special thing: it comes like a real-life film and shows me things that have already happened even if I wasn't there at the time. But it's always a surprise—I never know which bit of Backwards it will be. I have to make sure I stop so I don't go too far backwards though, because sometimes there are things there that I don't want to see.

My head is going woozy.

It's about to start . . .

Mum opens the shed door—she forgets you have to lift it up a bit and it scrapes on the grass and gets stuck halfway.

This bit of Backwards wasn't long ago. Mum's hair is red so maybe it was today, maybe yesterday; she was blonde until she went to the hairdresser's on Monday.

Her face has tidy make-up so it's in the morning before work. She's cross though.

'Where is the bloody thing?'

She kicks the watering can. She's wearing pointy leopard-patterned shoes.

The squiggles make my stomach funny. I can't look at them.

'Sure I had it somewhere.' She stands up with her hands on her hips, 'MIKEY! MIKEY! Where's the car toolbox? Bloody thing won't start. MIKEY?'

Chapter One

I can't remember her shouting at me this morning, or yesterday. I think I might have been out on a walk with Timmer. I wish I'd known the car wouldn't work—then I could have helped her to get it going again. I like helping.

She rummages around in the garden stuff—the watering can, the green hose, the plant pots. She puffs a bit under her breath.

'Hah! Gotcha.'

Mum pulls out the blue toolbox, flicks it open and takes out the jump leads. She sticks her neck out, looks further into the box. She's seen something else.

'Ohhhhhh!' she says, like a big happy sigh.

What's she found, Timmer? What's she found?

I shuffle forwards on my sunlounger-chair so I can see better.

Mum goes slow and soft for a moment and leaves the jump leads dangling over her arm. She smiles. Mum's beautiful when she smiles.

'Bless him.'

She holds it up.

Hey, look, Timmer—it's my old red Tonka truck! When I was little I used to play at mending it like I was a mechanic.

Mum spins one of the wheels with her long bright-pink nails.

She's useless with cars, Mum is.

She kisses the little truck and puts it back. 'My boy,' she whispers.

I go all squidgy and warm.

Bless him—that's me! I made her smile with my Tonka truck. Timmer wags his tail and looks up at me. He knows. He always understands.

Mum looks at her watch and groans. She walks back to the house, clicking her high heels up the path.

The swirly feeling is in my legs. I sink back into the suntan sunlounger-chair. If I close my eyes, everything still swims and it all smells of summer.

Some more Backwards is coming to show me something else that has happened in the shed. Not Mum this time. *Slow shuffles*. I frown. I nudge Timmer with my knee just in case. He pricks up his ears.

The door creaks open.

It's a man. An old man. A big floppy black hat. A dark coat—scrappy and dirty. I can smell him. He stinks of pee and parks and smoke. He looks inside, mouth open. He holds up his lighter and I can see his face. Dirty, with a bushy grey beard.

I yawn and lean back into the cushions. It's only the tramp. I haven't seen him in here for a while. I'm not sure when this was, but it's further into the Backwards. He's wearing a big jumper under his coat so maybe it was last winter. It's way too hot for all that stuff now. Timmer snuffles next to my leg.

6

Chapter One

After this one, we'll stop so we don't go too far back, Timmer. Don't worry.

He comes into the shed and hums under his breath— he's jerky when he moves. 'Shhhhhhhhh,' he says to the watering can, lifting his finger to his lips. 'Shhhhhhhhhhh, don't tell . . . '

I usually see him in the bus-shelter on the way to school, calling out from his newspaper nest like an old rook. He always tries to talk to me. I don't know why. Maybe it's because I'm always on my own. Mum says to make sure I keep away from him but it doesn't matter when I watch him in the Backwards because he can't see me. Mum doesn't believe that I can do that.

He starts to poke around on the workbench. The moonlight shines on his fingers—they are all wrinkly and the nails are thick and bumpy. He lifts up a ball of green garden string. He lets the dangly bit touch his hand. He smiles. I think he likes it soft on his skin. He sees the broken deckchair.

'Ahhh! Ha haaa!'

He eases himself down over the chair.

Don't sit on that, you stupid man. Can't you see it's broken?

He sticks his bum out and lets out a big sigh, like he's sinking into a hot bath. Then he lets himself drop.

'Ahhhhhhhh . . . '

The stripy deckchair fabric rips and the tramp falls

through the hole. Stupid fool! His surprised head, hat all wonky, is squashed up to his legs and his bum is on the floor.

He starts to laugh. A wheezy laugh.

Makes me laugh too. Old idiot!

He wriggles to pull his hip flask out of his pocket and takes a swig, sitting there, head-over-knees.

'Whoo hooo!'

He waggles his muddy boots in the air, yellow laces all tangly and undone.

'Whoo hooo!'

I clap and give him a round of applause.

He laughs again. 'Just came here to keep an eye on the lad, keep an eye on him . . . '

Keep an eye on who? Which lad? Me?

A cloud covers the moon outside and I hear a sudden crash from the house. I sit up. Timmer stands up and growls. Is this the Now or the Backwards? Is Mum all right? I put my hands over my eyes and concentrate. I can't hear anything except for the tramp and his jiggling in the broken deckchair.

The tramp hears something too though and stops moving. He frowns. He turns and looks straight at me.

'Oh no.' He shakes his head. 'Oh no!'

A hard fist squeezes in my belly.

'You can't see me, can you?' I ask him. People in the Backwards can never see me. He doesn't answer. The dark is getting darker.

Chapter One

The tramp struggles to get out of the deckchair. He wriggles really hard like a fat fish in a net. The deckchair falls on its side. He squirms out.

I hear another crash—the smashing of glass from the house? My head spins. My eyes ache. Is it Mum? In the Now? Is she OK? I stand up quickly. The floor goes topsy-whirly under my feet.

The tramp looks up.

'Stay away.' He puts up his hands. 'Stay away from me . . . '

He crawls back towards the door.

I hold my hands up. 'I'm not doing anything!'

I take a step towards him. I reach my hand out to him. **The tramp ignores me. He's not looking straight at me—he's looking at something behind me in the shed.** I try to hold onto his hand but I move straight through it like a ghost. Timmer growls and stands up.

'Stay here!' I whisper to the tramp. 'Don't go . . . '

He ignores me. The tramp is in a hurry now. He gets his coat stuck on the handle of some garden shears. He pulls hard to get it off—it rips but he doesn't care. He's shaking. He pushes the door open, but keeps looking just behind my head as he gets up. He backs out into the garden.

My stomach is all dead inside.

The shadows are waking up and they are hungry. There is only one person who comes to the shed and makes them like this.

I know who the tramp has seen.

I follow him to the door. I look up towards the house. The lights in the windows are twizzling—the house is swirly. I can't see inside properly. Timmer is next to me, leaning against my leg, growling. He is warm. I hold onto his collar very tight. I want to run to the house but I can't because he is here now.

He is here.

He is behind me.

I have gone too far Backwards.

Chapter Two

'Hello, Mikey.'

That sing-song quiet voice.

My legs go wobbly. I feel sick. I sit down hard on my sunlounger-chair and pull my knees under my chin. How did I let us go back this far, Timmer? What did I do wrong?

Timmer stands guard between me and him. Timmer's growl is so quiet that I can hardly hear it but every bit of my dog is tight and waiting waiting waiting. Backwards-Dad won't be able to see me sitting here but I still need Timmer with me more than anything in the world. My hands are slippery. I grab hold of Timmer's collar again. Stay close, boy. Stay close.

Dad is leaning against the workbench. I don't look up at his face. His boots are clumpy and big. I can't remember Dad being in the shed since, since . . . It makes me feel cold and hot all at the same time. I look for Little Mikey. I want him to stay hidden and safe. Which bit of the Backwards is this? Which bit? My fingers squeeze tight round Timmer's collar. I can't remember. That makes me frightened.

'I'm talking to you, Michael.'

Timmer looks up at me. He whines. Something is wrong.

'Can't you shut that dog up, Mikey? I am *trying* to talk to you.'

I look up. Dad is staring straight at me. He looks weird. Kind of brighter than everything else, even than the moonlight. He's not like I remember. Short hair—nearly shaved—and there's a bruise on his face. It's his eyes that are the worst. They are big and scared and teary and wild. I can't stop looking at them. They are sucking me in. I clench my teeth. I don't like it. I don't remember. When was this, Timmer? He can't hear you barking, can he?

'Michael?'

I look behind me but Little Mikey still isn't here. Who is Dad looking at? It's just me and Timmer.

'Mikey, it's me, Dad. Aren't you going to say hello?'

The dark of the shed presses against my head and my belly squeezes hard. This can't be right. *Dad can see us*. This is the *Backwards* and he's talking to me in the *Now*. My legs go all tight because they want to run as fast as they can.

'I've missed you, Mikey.'

Dad bends down next to me. His knees crack. He reaches out towards me. His hand is shaking. His face has lines with shadows in them. Timmer growls. There's a whooshing noise in my head.

'You miss me too?'

If I speak to him, it'll make this real. This is the Backwards, isn't it? I shuffle away from him. Dad leans forward. There's a sore line on his neck—a red, angry line. He's got this funny look on his face: I can't work out if he's mad or if he's going to cry. He reaches out to touch me but then stops. I hold my hands round my head.

'It's me! Just your old dad . . . '

I run my finger down the scar on the back of my head. A bump where my skin is stitched together.

'What d'you want?' I whisper.

'I wanted to see my boy again.' Dad's voice is crackly. I look up at him. His eyes are watery.

'How did you get out of prison?' My voice is little.

I want to lean forwards to him but I don't. Dad smells of the stuff Mum cleans the toilet with. I jump as his hand lands on the top of my head and ruffles my hair. His hand is strong and warm. My scar hurts. Timmer's ears flatten back, he snarls.

'Does it matter?' he whispers back.

'Are you here? Really here?'

Dad lifts up my face. His thumb strokes my cheek.

I go still. He chews his lip, opens his mouth to say something and then closes it. The bruise on his face is really big. His neck looks sore. I bet he's been fighting again. Dad clears his throat.

'I'm sort of outside things now, Mikey.'

'You escaped?'

He coughs. 'Kind of.' He says something but I can't hear him.

'Eh?'

'I said, I need to show you something, Mikey . . . '

My head swirls. Show me what? I can feel the Backwards pulling at me but it's dark and I don't want to see it, whatever it is. It smells bad. Dad clenches his fists like he's getting ready for something bad too.

I don't understand this. I don't understand it at all. I want to go home.

'I oughtta go back.' I pull at Timmer.

Dad flinches. 'You see me for the first time in years and you want to run straight back to Mummy?'

'She might need . . . I ought to go . . . ' My voice stops working.

'Stay a while, Mikey. Stay with your old dad . . . ' He sits down next to me.

He's too close. My head aches. The shed is getting smaller. The shadows are getting bigger. I close my eyes. Bruises. Fists. Shouting. I can't breathe.

I shake my head. 'I can't.'

Dad goes dead still. He picks up the chisel on the workbench and pushes it hard into the floor. Little curls of wood twirl out of it.

'I've come all this way and you're just going to leave me? Even though I made sure we could be all alone?'

Oh no. Timmer, stay close. Dad's upset. It's my fault.

'Mikey?'

I rock myself back and forth, back and forth. Shhhhh. Shhhhh.

He grabs my shoulders. Timmer stands up and growls. Dad gives a warning kick but Timmer is ready for it and dodges.

'I need you to STAY and WATCH, OK?'

I shake my head and move a bit further to the door. Dad stands up to get there first—he waits in front of it so I can't get out.

'I ASKED you to STAY, Mikey . . . It's important . . . Please!'

Dad grabs at me. I dodge out the way. Timmer jumps up to stop his arm. He snaps at Dad's shirt sleeve. Dad twirls round.

'Watch it, doggy!'

He kicks out at Timmer again. His back is to me. The door is open.

This is my chance.

I am running, running back towards the house. The arms of the bushes try to get me as I run past.

Timmer, come with me! Come on, boy!

I bang on the kitchen window. The dark of the garden presses on my back. Mum is kneeling on the floor. She's sweeping up smashed glass on the floor. She turns and looks confused. There's a drum banging in my ears.

'Let me in! The door's locked—let me in!'

Mum stands up, stumbles to the back door. I look behind me. I can't see anything. I can't hear anything from the shed. Where's Timmer? Where's Dad? Mum fumbles with the lock. Timmer, Timmer, come back to me. Come back!

I see a streak of animal run through the shadows. Timmer bounds up the garden towards me and stands, panting, next to me. I run my hand down his back. He's not hurt.

Where's Dad?

I look back to the shed. He is standing in the doorway, watching me. Why doesn't he come and get me? There is a long black shadow stretching from me all the way back to the shed. I can hear whispers in it. It isn't a dead shadow, it's alive. The night-garden is watching to see what will happen. I can't see his face. He starts to move.

'Mum! Hurry up!'

I bang on the door again. Why is she so sloooow? Dad's hand reaches out into the dark. Hurry, Mum, hurry! Still watching me, he pulls the shed door to him slowly, slowly slowly, until it clicks shut.

Mum opens the kitchen door. It's warm and light behind her.

'I didn't realize you were still out in the dark! Sorry, love.'

I push into the kitchen and half-fall onto Timmer's bean-bag.

'What was the panic? Careful—I just dropped my glass on the floor . . . '

I hold Timmer to me tight.

'You look like you've seen a ghost! Where have you been?'

Mum smiles down at me. She's been wobbling but she doesn't want me to know.

As she pulls the kitchen door shut, I hear a clanking noise from the shed.

I flinch.

It sounds just like a chisel, thrown to the floor.

Chapter Three

'Dad's escaped from prison and he's in the shed!'
My voice is all muffled because I'm trying not to cry.
I lean over my knees so my head is half-buried in my arms.
My trainers stick to the brown swirly lino on the floor.

'What?'

Mum sits down next to me and rubs my shoulders.
Her hands are so soft that I can hardly feel them through
my T-shirt.

'It's Dad! He's out! He's in the shed!'

Mum pushes a bit of my hair out of my face and hooks
it round my ear. She's trying to look calm but I can see her
hand is shaking a bit. 'You saw Dad?'

I nod. Snot is coming down my nose.

Mum pulls a scrunched-up tissue from up her sleeve
and hands it to me. 'In the shed?'

I nod again.

'Impossible, love.' She shakes her head. 'Wait here—
I'll go and see. Timmer, come with me!'

She's gone with my dog before I can say anything.
I try to stand but the kitchen winks with stars and my
legs won't work. I grab at the edge of the kitchen table
so I don't fall over. All the photos are still here, muddled
all over the table. Mum and Dad on their wedding day,
his chest puffed out, her face smiling like the sun. Mum
and me, when I was Little Mikey, making biscuits—I've
got a really big apron tied round me and I won't look at
the camera because I'm too busy shoving the biscuit mix
in my mouth. Me and Dad and Mum, sitting in a row on
the beach, hair all over the place . . . The Backwards is all
frozen in pictures.

'There's no one in the shed, love.' Mum is back in the
kitchen, a bit out of breath. She sees me looking at the
photos and snatches them out my hand and starts stuffing
them in an old brown envelope.

'But I saw him! He was talking to me!'

Mum takes hold of my hands. 'The shed's empty,
Mikey. Just the lawnmower and the toolbox and the other
gubbins in there.'

'NO!'

'*Yes*, Mikey. I've told you lots of times, love. Dad is
gone.' She squeezes my hands so I look up into her eyes.
She sighs. 'He's in prison for a long time.' Another squeeze.

'We have to *forget* about him. He isn't here for us any more so it's easiest not to think and talk about him. That's our Golden Rule, isn't it?' Her lips are shaking but her eyes won't let go of mine. 'OK, Mikey?'

'He spoke to me . . . '

'It's just your imagination again, Mikey. This has happened before.'

'NO! Not like this—I just *watched* him in the Backwards before but this time he *spoke* to me in the Now . . . He did! Timmer was there! He said he was on the outside now . . . '

Mum closes her eyes and puts her hands over her face. 'Not this Backwards stuff again, Mikey. Please.' She rubs her eyes with her hands and takes a deep breath. 'I know what it's like, sweetheart, since the accident . . . But this Backwards business has to stop . . . ' Her voice goes harder. 'It's not real, love. It's not good for you.'

'NO NO NO NO NO!' A black cloud is building up in my chest and is going to burst out of me and fill the whole room if she doesn't stop. 'I *saw* Dad. He spoke to me. He did!'

Mum's shoulders go down and she lets go of my hand. Her voice wobbles. 'Don't, Mikey. Just . . . ' She walks over to the sink and lights a fag, ' . . . don't.' Her whole face is crumpled like a screwed up bit of paper. 'I can't stand it. I just can't. Forget him. Just forget him. I can't keep talking about him . . . ' She turns to face the window and looks out into the night so I can't see her. 'I just can't,' she whispers.

I turn round. I can still see her face in the window: it's like a black mirror. She's crying and crying and crying with her mouth open but she won't let any sound come out because she thinks I can't see. The kitchen is so quiet. I hear the clock ticking on the fridge. I hear the freezer hum. Timmer shuffles and makes a nest on the bean-bag. Mum's crying and I feel empty. I'm supposed to look after her and look what I've just done. Look!

I take a step closer to her but I don't touch her. 'Sorry, Mum,' I whisper. 'I'm sorry.'

Mum turns a bit and she pulls me to her for a hug. I put my arms round her shoulders because I'm bigger than her now and she leans on me. We stand like that for ages. I know she's crying but I keep still and don't say anything because that's how I get her to stop.

''S all right, Mikey. 'S all right. It's just you and me now. You and me.' She rubs the top of my arm. 'Now, no more talk of . . . of . . . him, hey?'

'OK.' I bite my lip because I know she's still wobbly. 'Shall I ask Pat to come round, Mum?'

Pat is Mum's sister and she helps us sometimes when it's like this. Mum pulls away from me and stubs out the fag. 'Oh, there's no need. Don't worry about me, Mikey.

I'm fine.' She smiles her puffy-eye smile. 'You are sweet to ask though.'

I look over her head to the shed. It's a black black shape in the dark. I know that something is in there but I can't say anything. I can't make Mum cry again.

'Time to go to bed now, hey? Tomorrow's another day.'

I click my fingers at Timmer so he'll follow us upstairs.

'You're sure you don't want me to arrange for you to go to summer camp tomorrow? I can still call them before I go to work, you know.'

'Naah.' I hate that stuff. It's the summer holidays and I want to do what I want to do. 'Timmer and me are going for a long walk.'

Mum squeezes my shoulder. 'OK, love. I'm on earlies so I'll be back in the afternoon anyway.' She yawns.

'I hope the car starts properly tomorrow,' I say. I'm remembering the Backwards in the shed when Mum looked in the toolbox. 'So you don't have to use the jump leads again.'

'Yeah.' Mum rolls her eyes. 'That car took ages to start on Tuesday. I was late for work.' She ruffles my hair. 'And you were no good, Mikey! I needed your help but you were nowhere to be seen until I saw you and Timmer roaming around in the distance, up on Cackler's hill as I was driving to work. No good to your old mum, eh?'

She laughs and it makes me feel warm.

'You tell me next time and I'll get it started, Mum.' I stand taller. 'I'm good with jump leads.'

She smiles. 'OK, love. I didn't tell you on Tuesday because I knew you'd be upset you couldn't help me.' Her smile freezes and she frowns. 'How *did* you find out the car wouldn't start?'

'I saw it in the . . . ' *Backwards.* I'm about to say 'Backwards' but I can't because then she'll cry again and get all upset. I clear my throat instead. 'The shed told me you were looking in it. Places tell me their secrets.'

Mum looks at me for a long time and then shakes her head.

'You're a worry, Mikey. You're a worry. Maybe one of the neighbours saw me and told you about it? Was that it?'

I shrug. I don't like lots of questions. They make my head whizzy.

'OK, love.' Mum pats my arm. 'I think we're both getting tired now. Time for bed. When you go out for a walk with Timmer tomorrow, make sure you leave a picture-note to tell me where you are going.'

'OK.'

'And make sure you're back by lunchtime . . . '

I am the last one out the kitchen. Just as I flick off the light-switch, I see something in the window of the shed. A face. *His* face. My hand freezes on the door handle. He's watching me. *He's still there*. I wasn't making it up!

I look for Timmer. Here, boy! Timmer wags his tail and licks my hand. What to do, Timmer, what to do? I look up at the shed again.

But it's just an empty window now.

The face has gone.

Chapter Four

The radio crackles get right inside my head and wake me up. They snap at my waking-up-dreams like bitey teeth. I put my head under my pillow but I can still hear them. Mum has left the radio on in the kitchen and it's not tuned in properly. The noise is in my head and I can't get it out.

I get dressed and slam down the stairs to turn it off.

As soon as I open the kitchen door, the noise is so loud it scratches the back of my eyes. There's stuff everywhere and bags on the floor to trip me up and no clean spaces and spilled milk dripping off the table and noise, noise all over, all muddled up so I can't see anything and it's all tangled.

Got to get out. Got to GET OUT.

Timmer!

I need the quiet of the river. I need to think.

I grab my bait box from the fridge and rush outside fast fast fast. As soon as the door bangs shut behind me, it all goes softer. I squat down and catch my breath.

Outside is kinder than inside. Timmer barks and runs around in circles—he knows where I want to go. The sun is smooth on my face. When I am at the river, I can stretch out as far as I want.

Timmer gives a yap. Time to go. He rolls in the messy yellow grass in the garden and then leaps up again, looking at me. Time to go. Time to fish. Let's go.

Then I stop. I need the river but my fishing stuff is in the shed.

In the shed.

Where Dad was.

Timmer looks up and whines. Is it safe, Timmer? Can we go back in there? The shed looks different, just like a normal shed now. The branches of the bushes aren't like scrabbly arms any more. Mum checked it though, didn't she? It's empty now, she said. It's weird but when I walk towards it, the Backwards feels heavier, like a dark sack of shadows strapped to my back. Can I go inside? Is he there? Will he have come back?

I reach out to the door. It's shabby—the green paint is coming off and the ends of the door are raggedy. I pick at the paint and scrunch it between my fingers. I remember the chisel. I remember Dad last night standing in the door of the shed, watching me, watching me. Timmer looks up at me, head on one side, black ear flopping over. He would know if Dad was in there, wouldn't he? He always knows these things. Doesn't he?

Is it safe, Timmer? He sniffs the ground at the bottom of the door and whines. I bend down. He's showing me something. Frost. Frost on a hot summer day.

I back away. Perhaps we'll just go for a walk, Timmer. Perhaps we won't fish today. But they are *my* things in there. It's *my* shed.

I hear a shout from next door. A door slams open.

'We need two loaves of bread and some milk!'

'Gotcha!'

Gavin'n'Tina, Tina'n'Gavin. Always talking about food. It feels safer to hear people around. I hear her run, clippety-clop heels, up the side of her house. The car door slams. The engine starts up. A Mazda 323. Gavin opens the upstairs window. Thud thud thud. His stompy music starts. THUD THUD THUD.

I hold my head. I have to think quick before Gavin's noise muddles me. I want the quiet of the river—I can feel it underneath the thudding. Timmer is here. Gavin is next door. I am not alone. THUD THUD THUD. I ache for quiet.

A blackbird lands on the branch of the apple tree next to the shed. He's often near me. Cheery little bird. He cocks his head to one side, asking what we're up to. Going

27

fishing, Blackie. Is it safe in there? Is it safe? The black-bird hops a little closer down to a branch closer to the door. There's my answer.

I pull the door open.

Timmer pushes past me and goes in first. He sniffs the air but he doesn't put his ears flat. It smells funny. Toilet cleaner smell? Or lawnmower smell? I don't know. I can't see nothing unusual. I think, think, it's empty.

I'm not taking any chances though.

I can reach the fishing bag and the rods from the door-way. I hold the door open with one hand. I push Timmer forward with my knee so I get hold of the bag handles. He steps further into the shed and looks up at me. He wonders what I want him to do.

Nothing, Timmer. Just be here with me.

I pull out the bag first with my other hand, then feel for the rods. My throat is tight. It's all right, Mikey, all right. My head is starting to hurt. It feels like there is something behind me I can't see. I spin round—just the garden, just the garden. It seems so bright and far away from in here.

Timmer growls. The shadows in the corner of the shed have got darker. I pull at the rod and nearly snap it to get it out into the sunshine extra-quick. The bottom of the rod hits something on the floor. It's the chisel. The floor goes topsy-whirly and I can hear someone laughing in my head.

The chisel points across the floor like an arrow. I can see the curly wood shavings. I see something shift out the corner of my eye. Behind the broken deckchair. Can't see it properly. Timmer growls again. The air feels thunderstorm-heavy. It's watching me. I yank the fishing stuff out the door. As the door closes, I see a flicker of something. A shadow moves. I've woken something up.

I run.

Once we're through the hole in the fence at the bottom of the garden, we're in the scrubland-before-the-fields. It's full of empty bottles and cans and plastic bags blowing about.

'And Jim Baker scores again!'

I turn round. It's the lads from the normal school playing footie. Jim and Toby and Dave. Jim is running around the others, arms in the air, T-shirt tied round his head.

'That doesn't count! We're just messing around—two against one isn't fair!' Dave is shouting but he's laughing too.

Dave will be the odd-one-out, I bet. He's standing between two bags on the floor, the goal. Toby does whatever Jim wants because he's the leader and he follows him everywhere. Toby and Jim will be the two-team.

'A goal is a goal is a goal!' Jim turns and wiggles his bum at them.

'Yeah!' Toby snorts and claps. 'Go, Jim!'

'Hey, there's Mikey!' Dave waves over at me. 'Fancy joining my team, Mikey-boy?'

Jim says something I can't hear. Toby holds his sides and starts laughing. Dave smiles and walks over to me. He's got a sunny face. The ground scuffs up around his feet because it's dry. Jim kicks dirt at him as he overtakes Dave.

'Nah! Mikey's going fishing, ain't yer?' He nods at my fishing rods.

'Yeah, but I can . . . ' I start to talk but Jim shakes his head and holds up his hand to me.

'And Dave,' Jim turns round and winks at him, 'you ought to know that Mikey-Mikey here needs slooooooooooooooooooow sports. Don't you, mate?'

Toby catches up. He puts his hands on his hips, then bursts out laughing again.

I look down. Timmer sits down on my feet. *I'm here*, he's saying to me. My chest feels funny. I swallow hard.

'Hey, catch this!' Toby throws the ball to Jim. Jim runs and kicks it back towards their bags. They both chase it and try to trip each other up as they go.

Dave punches my arm. 'Take no notice, Mikey. We were just finishing here anyhow. They're just arsing about cos it's the beginning of the holidays.'

Jim kicks the ball through the bags and lets out a whoop.

Chapter Four

'ANOTHER goal for Jim Baker!' He punches the air.

Dave rolls his eyes at me and walks back to his friends, slow-clapping. I look down at Timmer. It's just me and you again, Timmer. Just me and you.

Chapter Five

I pull my knees up under my chin and watch the river go by. The sun is hot on my back. She is fast today. I can't see the bottom. The water goes deep and then hides things. It's been hot for ages so I bet the fish are getting sleepy. There are barbel in this stretch of river—they like hiding in slacks here behind the weed beds. I worked out this is one of their swims and caught loads of them but they're getting to know my bait. I ought to change it soon. I like it here though—when I'm sitting down, it's hard to see me because of the high reeds. No one else ever comes here.

There's a good spot just up near the willow tree but I never fish there because it feels full of shadows, so I'll have to find somewhere else.

Timmer runs down the bank and drinks a bit of water

and turns to me wagging his tail, ears forward. Not today, Timmer-dog. No playing today. I pull my knees tighter. I want to hold myself small and neat. I dig the toe of my trainer into the grass. I forgot my fishing umbrella to make some shade and my T-shirt is starting to stick to my back.

Timmer flops down next to me. He's smiling, tongue hanging out. He's river-muddy, dark brown all up his legs to the long furry bit on his belly. He rolls onto his back. I'm not stroking you when you're that mucky, Timmer-dog! He snuffles and lies still. Timmer gets quiet here too.

The river is listening. She never speaks, just listens. It makes me feel better but I don't know why. Mr Oldfield at school says that rivers go all the way to the sea. They start as little dribbles high at the top of a hill and then get bigger and bigger as they go on and on and then the sea swallows them up. I like it that the river always goes forwards. I like that it goes to the sea, the sea, the sea. Always forwards, never backwards.

Something catches my eye on the other side of the river in the reed bed. Ahhhh! She's here—my special bird. The bittern. I hold Timmer's muzzle so he's quiet. She's beautiful—a long curvy neck—and shy. She only comes out if she feels safe. She fishes with me in the river, sometimes. I reckon she's got a nest over there in all the reeds somewhere. I keep still and quiet with Timmer. We stay like that for ages.

Slowly, she walks out, neck stretched. I don't move.

She stands still—waiting, watching. She leans forward. There's something in the water. Another step. Darts forward. Jabs the water. Pulls back, neck high. She's eaten. Then she's gone, back into the rushes, lifting her big feet carefully as she goes.

I smile. She's my secret. Mum says the bitterns have only just come to live in this reed bed. My bittern never makes a noise. Lots of people have heard the he-bittern making his special booming noise but no one else has seen one because bitterns like to hide. No one has seen one here. No one except me.

I can breathe again: the outside magic has worked. I can think about last night now my head is better. I lean back on my elbows, sun on my face. Was Dad *really* in the shed? Or did I do something different to make the Backwards go funny? Timmer shuffles to get closer to me and sits on the extra bit of fishing line. I pull a bit out and wrap it round my hand. I cut off the end of the bit of fishing line with my penknife and lay it down on the grass. It looks like the line in a school book. I want to think along it to keep things straight.

How do I watch the Backwards, Timmer? What happens?

1. I feel when the shed has a secret it wants to tell me. I just sit and wait for it, like I'm fishing and waiting for a fish. That's what I did last night. I just sat on the sunlounger chair and waited.

I cut off some more fishing line and put it under the first bit. What next?

2. The world swirls and then it starts. The Backwards people come. They just do. That's what happened last night until . . . until Dad came . . . until he chased the Backwards tramp away.

I frown. I don't understand. How could Backwards-Dad chase the tramp away in a different bit of Backwards? More fishing line.

3. I see secrets. People come back to the same place and I see what they were up to: a real-life film just for me.

All these things are true. And I was the same as usual last night. I watched the tramp, didn't I? And Mum? It was all right until Dad came—but, before last night, even if I went too far back by mistake, I only watched it.

I cut another bit of line and lay it down straight beneath the other ones.

4. I watch. I listen. But I don't speak to them. Never. And they don't speak to me.

Until now.

I look at the bits of fishing line on the grass—four stupid lines for stupid Mikey who can't work anything out ever. I scrunch them up and throw them into the fishing-bag. The river keeps on going. Dark and quiet and full of secrets. My head aches.

Timmer barks. There is someone behind me. A shadow falls on the grass.

'You want to watch that fishing line—you nearly got one there.'

I squint upwards. There is a man standing next to me, blocking out the sun.

'Eh?'

He points to my fishing rod.

'Yer line, mate. You want to watch it.'

He's that farm bloke from Cackler's Farm. He's about as tall as Dad. Same age too. Big muscles. Drives a tractor. He's carrying a bag of tools and some wire. Looks like he's going to mend the fence on the other side of the field.

I stand up. I am nearly as tall as him, but he looks bigger and stronger than me.

'Dunno you'll have much success.'

He looks at me out of the corner of his eye. He's got brown eyes. They look nervous, like an animal when it's sussing you out. I might talk to him. Maybe. He looks back to the river and holds his hand to his eyes to shade the sun—he's got a tattoo of a naked woman on the top of his arm.

'You been 'ere before, en't you?'

The woman has long hair and is kneeling down. Curves. Lots of curves.

'I'm sure I seen you with that dog.'

He looks at me. I look at the curvy naked lady. Does it feel different with a woman on your arm? Not just the paint or whatever it is, but because a woman is there, under your skin. Naked and curvy. He waits and looks back at the river.

'Quiet, ain't yer? Place for quiet people here though I reckon.'

He watches the float bob bob bobbing on the river. People never usually do that. Just stand and watch next to me. He keeps looking at me but I don't know what to say. He fiddles with the catch on his belt—maybe I'm making him nervous. I stay quiet.

'Hey, what's that?' He points to the rushes downstream, just in the bend of the river.

I can't see anything. There's something funny where he's pointing though. I go cold and shivery.

'Was it a bittern?' He looks at me. 'Cackler said there are some round here. He hasn't drained that field especially to keep the reed-bed.'

I shift from one foot to the other. He mustn't go there. It's not all right.

He's watching me now. 'Can you see it?' He waits.

I don't want him to look at it. If she *is* there, she might have little bitterns and there'll be no he-bittern to help her protect them. This man has to leave her alone. She's my secret.

I don't trust men and little things. He leans close to me like he's looking for something in me. I wrinkle my nose and clench my fists. He laughs but his eyes still stare at me a bit longer.

'Come over here, I'll show you.'

He starts to walk downstream a few paces. Shadows wake up in the long grass. If I had just spoken to him I could have kept him here with my fishing rod, not going off looking for my bittern.

'Stop!'

My voice squeaks.

The man turns round.

'Eh? D'ya say something, mate?'

'Stop.' My voice is deeper this time. Sounds more of a man's voice. 'Please.'

'Ah, so you know it's a bittern.' The man taps the side of his nose. 'Don't need to worry about me, mate. I'll be as quiet as a mouse. Just take a peek. Country man me. Won't disturb 'em.'

He walks away, great big wellies thundering along. Some bloody mouse. He'll upset them. You can't get too close.

'Stop!'

I shout again and follow him. This bit of riverbank doesn't feel calm like the bittern's place. It feels cold and black and whispery. I scrunch my T-shirt in my hands. Timmer bounds up and gallops round me, all excited like. We're not going on a walk, stupid, we're trying to stop that clod-hopping-curvy-naked-woman man.

He has stopped. I nearly bump into him. Timmer whimpers.

Chapter Five

'What's that?'

The man points to a dark shape by the water this side of the riverbank. There is a quiet all around it: I have never known anything so quiet. The river goes by but she knows too. This is another of her secrets that goes down into the dark deep. I don't know how but I know this secret. I know the dark shape. The man looks at me, eyes wide.

'Can you see that, mate?'

I take a step forward. Timmer stays close to my legs. He nearly trips me up. My head feels under water because I can't hear properly any more. There's a gap in the reeds and I can see a boot. A muddy boot. Yellow laces. The field and the river spin round and round me but the boot stays still. I don't need to go any further.

'I know . . . ' I start but my voice cracks.

The man grabs my arm. 'You know who it is?'

His face is close but it's all blurry and all I can see properly is that boot. The muddy boots. They were poking through the broken deckchair in my shed last night. Waggling because he got stuck.

The man runs down the riverbank. He shouts at me but I can't hear him. My legs won't work and I flop down onto the grass. He's waving his hands. The wind blows the reeds. The sky has gone dark. I am cold. The man is bending down now, waving at me to go over to him again. I shake my head. I can't move. I know who it is.

'It's the tramp.'

My words hang there. The man's mouth drops open. He steps to one side, pulling the reeds with him. He's watching me with this strange strange look on his face. He's almost smiling. I can see the dark shape without moving any closer to the river. A wrinkly dirty hand holds the black floppy hat. The tramp's face is turned to the other side of the riverbank and I only see a bit of purple cheek. The beard floats into the water. The body rests on the reeds—it belongs to the river now.

My head is black. The man walks over, tall tall above me. I close my eyes. I don't want to see any more. I wrap my arms round my head and hide my face in my knees. The bump of my scar is sore. The Backwards is pulling and pulling at it. I can't stand the shadows here. I groan. Timmer leans right up to me.

The man puts his hand on my shoulder. I feel the growls in Timmer's body and the man pulls his hand away again.

'You knew the tramp's body was in the river?' His mouth is right next to my ear. The words hiss in my head. 'You knew?'

I nod. I did. But I don't know how I knew. Maybe the river told me. Maybe the bittern told me. Maybe it was the Backwards whispering in my head.

The man steps back. I look at him through my fingers. He's got that weird smile on his face again. It looks like a trap.

'You stay here, right?' His voice is sharp. 'I'm going for help.'

I don't move.

'You hear me? I can't get a reception on my mobile here.' He waits. 'What's your name, mate?'

'Mikey.'

I still don't move.

The man steps towards me again. Timmer lets out a loud growl.

'I'll be back soon, OK? Just stay here, mate. Stay here . . . '

He walks back to the river. I lift my head up and watch him go. He rubs the back of his head—he's thinking about something—stops and turns round. He's in front of the sun so I can only see his dark shape. Then he starts walking again, up the path to the farm.

I feel the river. I stand up and walk over to it. I crouch down and let it pull my fingers. I was right. There are bad secrets here. He hasn't got any forwards now, the tramp, only Backwards. No more forwards. What happened to you, tramp? What happened?

I look out across the fields on the other side of the river. Marshy reed fields that go up to the farm buildings on Cackler's farm. The trees at the edge of the field bend a bit. The wind is shaking them. It sends squiggly patterns across the river. It talks to me in a mean and whispery voice.

You saw the tramp last night, it says. *Even in the Backwards, he was frightened of your dad. You know because you were there. You saw it, didn't you? Then Dad got angry. YOU made Dad angry. And look, Mikey-Mikey, loooooook . . .* The wind blows grit into my face so that my eyes sting. *Looook and seeeee what happened to the tramp . . .*

All the world is still. All the world is cold. There is frost on the ground, biting at me.

Frost again?

It crunches when I stand up. It winks in the sunlight. It leads all the way to the tramp. I put my hands under my armpits to get warm. The wind blows at my back, pushing me towards him. I can't feel a thing because the frost is so cold.

There he lies. I can see him better now the farm-man has gone. It's funny but he doesn't look like the tramp any more. Something has gone so it isn't really him now. The frost twinkles like stars on his coat. Black smoke is starting to puff out of his head. Smoke from the Backwards. The world swirls.

I've never seen black smoke like this before. I don't like it. I don't like it at all. I close my eyes. The frost snaps at me until I open them again. I have to watch this.

The black tramp-head smoke makes a cloud. It spreads out and hangs above him along the river like bad mist. Inside I feel as if I've run and run and run and am about to burst. There are little pictures in the mist. Little bits of Backwards.

The moon is high in the sky. The tramp swigs from a bottle. Moonlight is beautiful on the water. Someone is behind the tramp. The bottle falls. The tramp's shoes are running. Everything is going down and black. Boots are kicking. Boots are kicking. Boots are kicking.

Big boots.

Heavy boots.

Dad's boots.

I stand up and run up the bank. I don't care about the black smoke, or the frost or the tramp. The world is spinning but I grab the fishing stuff and start to run. I run out of the Backwards, out of the frost. I feel the summer sun on my arms but I keep going. Faster, Mikey, faster, faster, faster.

You have to get back to Mum.

Hurry, Mikey, hurry.

You have to make sure she's safe.

Chapter Six

'Mum, you've got to listen to me . . .' I'm out of breath from running. She's home from work now. She's at the kitchen table, pressing the numbers on the telephone. She looks up, sees me, and puts the phone down. She rolls her eyes and lets her hands drop on the table.

'Where did you *go*, Mikey? How many times do I have to tell you to leave a note?'

'Mum, listen! Something's happened . . . we have to . . .'

'And that dog is filthy! He stinks—wash him down before you let him in the house *please*!' She looks at Timmer and points at the door. 'You! Out!'

Timmer puts his tail between his legs.

'MUM! I'm sorry but this is important!'

'So is telling me where you are, Mikey!' She stares at Timmer until he's gone. 'How many times . . . ? Do you realize how worried I was?'

She isn't listening to me and it's important. I sit down at the table and hold one of her hands. If I hold her hand she'll listen to me. She loves it when I do that. Mum starts to smile even though she's trying not to.

'Don't cry when I tell you this? Promise?'

Her nails dig into my hand. She frowns.

'What, Mikey?'

'It's the tramp.'

'The tramp? Which tramp? The . . . the bus-shelter tramp?'

'Yeah.' I take a deep breath. 'He's dead. By the river.'

'Dead?' She bites her lip. 'How do you . . . oh, you, you've been fishing down the river? He was . . . '

I nod.

'Oh God!' She stands up and all her gold bangles jangle down her arm. She squeezes me. 'You OK? You see him?'

I nod again.

'He was definitely . . . I mean you got near to . . . he wasn't sleeping rough?'

I think for a minute. I know what she's asking. She wants to make sure he really is dead. How can I tell her why I knew he was dead? I just knew. The farm-man did too.

'His face was in the water—the bruises . . . '

'Oh, Mikey.' She reaches out to rub the top of my arm.

'You poor thing, you . . . It's OK. I'll call the police. They'll take care of it. It's not for you to worry about any more.'

'He's already called them.'

She stops rubbing my arm. 'Who has?'

'The man.'

'Which man?'

'The farm-man from Cackler's farm.'

'He was there too?'

I close my eyes because the questions are coming too quick but it's OK because it's Mum and she's not trying to trap me. Not like the farm-man. 'Yes, the man found the tramp but I already knew he was there.'

'What?' Mum's face is sharp.

'I told the man I knew the tramp was there. I just knew. I don't know how.'

Mum sits down slowly.

'That's OK isn't it, Mum? Mum?'

'How did you know the tramp was there, Mikey?' Her voice is really quiet. I don't like it.

'I don't know, I . . . I just knew.'

Mum runs her hands across the table like she's smoothing out some wrinkles that I can't see. Timmer patters back into the kitchen.

'And you told the man this while you were fishing and then he found the body?'

I nod.

'And then he left to call the police?'

'Yes.'

Mum's hand flies to her mouth. She breathes in quick.

She leans forwards and takes my hand. 'Look, Mikey, I won't be cross, but you have to tell me the truth OK? This is really important.'

My head is going all dark and swirly again. Think, Mikey, think. Mum says this is important. I look into her eyes. They are blue blue blue.

'How did you know the tramp was there?'

I can't say the Backwards because she'll cry. 'I dunno. I just did.'

She looks away, coughs, and then looks back at me. 'You didn't, you didn't have anything to do with it?'

'NO!'

I jump up. My chair falls over, nearly hits Timmer. This is wrong! This is wrong! Does the farm-man think I did something bad? Timmer, Timmer, stop barking! Why does he think that? This is all slipping the wrong way. I had something I had to tell Mum. The black smoke. The kicking in the Backwards. I knock my knuckles against my head hard to get the words straight to tell her.

'NO, NO, NO!'

'I'm sorry, Mikey.' She stands up and puts her arms round me to keep me still. 'I just wanted to check, I just wanted to make sure . . .' She waits for me to stop moving, 'I know you're a good lad but sometimes people misunderstand . . . misunderstand things . . . '

'I was just fishing.'

'Of course you were.'

'But I wanted to tell you, I wanted to tell you . . . '

'What, love?'

I am glad I don't have to see her face when I say it. I push my face in her hair. It tickles.

'Dad killed him.'

Mum doesn't say anything. She goes still. Timmer whines. I hear Gavin next-door start the lawnmower up.

'I saw him—well, some of him like I saw him in the shed last night. Mum, what are we going to do?'

Gavin's lawnmower drones on. It's loud because the window is open. When Mum speaks, her voice sounds far away.

'Your dad's still in prison, Mikey. He hasn't escaped. We checked the shed last night, remember? It was empty.'

'The Backwards showed me . . . '

She pushes me away. I feel cold.

'I thought we talked about this yesterday.' Mum's mouth goes into a straight line and she holds one hand on her forehead.

'NO! That's not fair! It's REAL!'

Mum closes her eyes and when she starts to talk, she's really quiet. 'Mikey, promise me, PROMISE ME, you'll stop this. PROMISE ME. This is important. Or I'll have to take you to the doctor's to help you to stop.'

'NO!!!!!'

I pull my hair hard hard hard hard hard . . . Mum grabs hold of my arms and her nails dig in deep. I wriggle but she won't let go.

'Mikey! I know you don't like it, but the doctors are only trying to help you.' She grips tighter and makes me look at her. 'This Backwards stuff is playing games with your head and it's not fair on you.' Her voice is soft now. 'You know I only want you to be happy, don't you? Yes, Mikey?'

Yes? Am I making all this up? Is it all in my head? Timmer pushes into my hand and licks it. But Timmer knows when the Backwards is coming, doesn't he? It's not just me, is it? Timmer grunts. He's there with me. It's real, I know it is.

'Mikey? Promise me you'll stop? I'm only trying to help.'

I hear a car pull up into the drive. I hear Gavin's lawnmower. I see the tramp's boots with the yellow laces floating in the water. I see the boots in the Backwards kicking, kicking, kicking. The doorbell rings.

Mum leans towards the door to see who it is and groans again.

Her mouth starts to tremble. 'Whatever they ask you, don't mention the stuff you see when you go funny—this Backwards business.'

I look up and her face is all blurry.

The doorbell rings again.

'Mikey? Oh God. MIKEY? Promise me you won't mention Dad to them either? Remember our Golden Rule?'

Ringgggggggggg.

All the sounds muddle and swirl.

'I'm coming!' Mum sounds bright and not like Mum and then she leans forwards and whispers, 'Promise me, Mikey.'

I nod to make her smile but I don't really know. Timmer whines again.

'And take that bloody dog back outside until he's clean . . . The watering can is full—it's under the outside tap.'

I drag Timmer outside again and start to pour water from the watering can down his legs. All the river-mud goes wet and slides down onto the grass. His legs shake when I do that and he pulls away from me so I have to hold his collar tight. He looks smaller when he's wet.

I hear a man's voice as Mum opens the front door.

'Mrs Baxter? Mrs Lisa Baxter? Detective Sergeant Carson. Could we step inside for a moment, please? We wonder if we could have a word with your son, Michael.'

I stand and watch from the lounge doorway. Mum pulls the old newspapers and magazines off the settee and tries to puff up the skinny blue cushion but it just stays skinny. Her face has gone all red to match her new hair and she's moving too fast.

'Take a seat, Sergeant . . . Sergeant . . . '

'Carson.' The policeman holds out his hand. He's about as tall as Mum but he's grey and a bit bald. His dark green jacket is open and his fat belly pushes at the shirt buttons. He may be wearing different clothes but I know he's still really a black-and-white.

Mum brushes her hair out of her face and holds out her hand. It looks all white and floppy like a dead fish.

'And this is Constable Jones.'

'Pleased to meet you.'

She shakes his hand too. He's really tall and thin and has loads of spots. His black-and-white policeman's clothes look like a too-big fancy dress outfit.

Mum sits right at the edge of the easy chair and the black-and-whites sit on the settee. There's nowhere for me to go.

'Bring in the kitchen chair, love,' Mum says.

'Ah, this must be Michael!' Sergeant Carson stands up again and shakes my hand too. It's a strong handshake. I smile. He raises his big bushy eyebrows but his eyes aren't too scary.

I put my chair in front of the fire but then I wish I hadn't because I'm opposite all the black-and-whites. Timmer knows I'm feeling a bit shaky and he comes and

51

sits at my feet. He's still wet and smells a bit but he has to stay with me, he has to. I push my fingers into the fur on his neck. Mum frowns at me and gets up to shoo Timmer away but Sergeant Carson holds up his hand.

'He can stay as long as he's no bother.'

Constable Jones makes a huffing noise. Mum raises her eyebrows at me—that means 'watch it'—and sits down again.

'We are here because we received a call about you this morning.' Sergeant Carson smiles but it's a be-careful-son smile. 'We'd like to ask you a few questions if that's OK.'

Constable Jones nods and pulls out a notebook. He looks at his watch and writes something down.

'Your mum says you're fourteen?' Sergeant Carson asks.

I nod. Constable Jones writes in his book again.

Sergeant Carson smiles. 'Could you tell us where you were this morning?'

I try to speak but my voice just squeaks. I swallow hard. Mum pulls a tissue out from her sleeve and twists it but her mouth stretches into a little smile. I try again.

'I went fishing.'

'What time was that?'

I swallow again but there's a lump in my throat and it won't go down. I can't work out the time. My head is starting to go fuzzy. I grab hold of the chair.

Mum clears her throat and speaks instead.

'Mikey goes to the special school down Peter's Street.'

She looks hard at Sergeant Carson. 'He was still asleep in bed when I left the house at eight o'clock.'

'You checked on him, Mrs Baxter?'

'Yes.'

'Do you remember seeing anyone this morning, Michael, on your way fishing?'

My fingers are so slippery they slide off the chair. I screw up my face. Everyone is looking at me and the room is going little. I close my eyes so they go away. This morning . . . I remember the radio noise . . . and the shadows in the shed . . . and then it was all right and I could go in because people were around. I open my eyes.

'I heard Gavin'n'Tina talking about shopping and Tina went for the bread and milk when I was in the garden getting my fishing rods.'

Sergeant Carson smiles. 'Thank you, Michael. That's very helpful.'

A fizzy excited feeling whizzes in my head like a mini-firework. I was helpful! To a policeman! A proper one. I smile back really hard. Sergeant Carson coughs.

'Tell me about when you got to the river, son.'

'I wanted some quiet so I sat still up near the bridge and did some fishing.'

'And what did you see?'

I bite my lip.

'Well, it's a secret.'

The black-and-whites sit up straight and Mum sort of jumps. Sergeant Carson speaks in a quiet voice but his eyes have come to life.

'It's better you tell us about it, son.'

Mum opens her mouth but he holds up his hand to her and keeps staring at me.

'Do you promise you won't hurt her?' I whisper.

'Her? Who's that, son?'

I wriggle on my seat. 'Promise? I sort of look out for her.'

'We're not in the habit of hurting people, Michael, but it's very important you tell us who you are talking about.'

I can feel her quiet in my head.

'Michael?' Sergeant Carson is looking at me. 'We need you to tell us this to help us. You are doing a very important job here, son.'

'The bittern,' I whisper.

'Ahhhhhh.' Sergeant Carson leans back, a little smile on his face. His eyes go a bit softer.

'Eh?' The skinny constable looks up.

'A bittern. A bird, Jones, a bird. Looks like a small heron. Endangered species.' The sergeant talks to me again. 'We won't hurt her, son. This secret is safe with us.'

My shoulders go down and I can breathe better.

'Tell me what else you found in the river today, Michael.'

54

'That farm-man turned up and we found the tramp's body when he was looking up the river.' My voice has gone quiet again.

'Yes. You found it together?'

'He saw it first.'

'The farm-man?' The sergeant raises his eyebrows. 'But he tells us that you knew it was there already.'

I remember the crackling frost leading me along the riverbank. I can see the farm-man and his strange smile as he pulls the reeds aside.

'He moved the grass by the river so I could see his boot.'

'You recognized the boot?'

I nod. There they are, sticking in the air out of the broken deckchair. My eyes sting. I press my lips together because they are starting to shake. Mum reaches out to me and touches my hand.

'Mikey passed the tramp sitting in the old bus-shelter every day on the way to school, didn't you, love?' Mum smiles at me.

I nod again. And sometimes he used to come and keep an eye on me in the shed—like the bit of Backwards I just saw last night. There's a drip at the end of my nose and it wobbles when I move my head. Mum passes me her tissue.

'And that's why you knew who the tramp was?'

'Yes.'

'What was it about the boots, son?' Sergeant Carson leans forwards to block Mum out a bit.

'Yellow laces,' I whisper.

He sits back, nodding, but doesn't say anything.

'Can I ask where you were last night, Michael?'

'He was here with me all night.' Mum pushes her hair out her face and smiles at the black-and-whites.

'I was asking your son, madam. If you don't mind . . .'

'I *was* here.' It's true. I was here in the shed.

'Just an ordinary gentle evening and then we had a chat just before we went up to bed, didn't we, love? I would say we went up . . . ooooo . . . about ten thirty.' Mum smiles again.

The sergeant frowns at her and looks at me with his eyebrows up.

''S true,' I say and smile at her.

Mum turns to Sergeant Carson.

'Is that when the tramp was killed, Sergeant? Last night?'

'Yes, madam. We think so but of course we'll have to wait for the results from the autopsy to confirm.' He stands up and his knees crack. He holds out his hand to Mum again. 'Thank you both for your time.'

Mum still has the too-bright smile on her face. 'Our pleasure, Sergeant.' She moves towards the lounge door with her arm out, pointing the way.

Detective Sergeant Carson bites his lip, watching me.

'You were very helpful, young man.'

He shakes my hand, too, like I'm a proper man. I stand extra-straight. The two black-and-whites go.

Mum comes back in, hands on hips, and blows hard out of her mouth. She goes to the kitchen and comes back with a beer in her hand. She takes a swig.

'God, what a day.' She runs her hands through her hair and flops onto the settee with her feet up on the coffee table.

'Is it all right, Mum? Are we in trouble?' I sit next to her.

She downs some more beer. 'No, love. You were brilliant.' She puts the beer onto the coffee table. 'No thanks to that bloody farm-man—dobbing us in like that. Should mind his own bloody business.'

'Dobbing us in?' The farm-man phoned up the black-and-whites and said I was up to no good with the tramp? 'He thinks I'm a bad 'un?'

Mum gives a big sigh, sags back into the sofa and closes her eyes.

'Maybe, love, but who cares, hey? Who cares? All's well that ends well.'

I remember how the farm-man stood next to me and was quiet when I was fishing. No one has been fishing with me since Dad was here and he thinks I'm a bad 'un. The tramp is dead. Dad has escaped. Timmer whines and pushes his nose into my leg. You're the only one that believes me, Timmer-dog. The only one.

'Hey!'

Mum reaches over to me and wipes my cheek. It's wet but I didn't notice. I close my eyes.

'You've had a rough few days, haven't you? Tell you what, let's plan a little treat. Just you and me. What do you want to do? Anything you fancy?'

Behind my eyes, the river is flowing forwards forwards forwards to the sea. In the photo of me and Mum and Dad, we were all happy and smiling when we went there. I open my eyes.

'Let's go to the beach!'

Mum lifts her head, eyebrows up. 'The beach? Like when you were little?'

'Yeah!' I jiggle my feet on the floor. 'Pleeeeeeeeease, Mum! You said I could choose! You just said it!'

Mum smiles a sad smile. 'OK. I've got a day off on Tuesday. Why not?'

My feet keep on jiggling. The beach! My treat! Did you hear that, Timmer-dog? Did you hear?

Chapter Seven

I wake up and my head is clear. I know what I'm going to do. I'm going to go to Cackler's farm to tell the farm-man I'm not a bad 'un. When I open the curtains in my room, the sky is like my head—blue all over, no clouds at all.

This is my bedroom, not Little Mikey's. He had the little front bedroom next to Mum's room. There's dark Backwards from long ago in that room—I won't go in there because it will show me scary things, so Mum let me move in here when Dad went away. It's much bigger and Timmer has a bed in here too.

There are two windows in my bedroom. The one at the front faces out onto the road. If you look really hard and scrunch up your eyes, you can see the fields at the edges of our estate but mostly it's just houses. I get a bit panicky if I can't see lots of green things and I don't like all the noise and people being able to look in, so I always keep the curtains shut on that window. They are orange so my room is always orange too and that makes it feel warm, even in the winter when the heating is dodgy. The back window is my favourite window and I normally have those curtains open all the time so I can see down the garden, the scrubland-before-the-fields and up to the fields and trees and river and reeds and farm.

I closed the curtains on the back window last night though. I don't care what Mum says—there was something in the shed, hugging its secrets and watching me so I couldn't sleep.

'Are you up yet, Mikey?' Mum's not at work until this afternoon so she'll make me breakfast today.

I run down the stairs, two at a time. Timmer flies down with me.

'Steady, Mikey!' Mum calls from the kitchen. 'Such a bloody racket!'

I don't take any notice and blast into the kitchen and give her a hug. She's standing at the sink, washing up with her pink rubber gloves on.

'You're in a good mood!' She flicks some washing-up bubbles at me.

They hang in the air for a minute. There are little rainbows caught in the middle of them. I pop one on my finger. Today is going to be such a good day! I wiggle my bum and twirl to make Mum smile.

'Get along with you, you silly oaf!'

She takes her gloves off and whacks me on the bum with them but she's laughing.

'No rest for the wicked—I'm cleaning today. You going out with Timmer?' She ruffles my hair as she goes by.

'Yeah.' I tip a load of Timmer's biscuits into his bowl. His head is in the way because he can't get at them fast enough and some of them spill on the floor. Doesn't matter. He'll hoover them up in no time.

'Make sure you're back for lunch, hey?' She gives me an extra-hard stare.

'OK.'

I stuff down the scrambled eggs on toast Mum's made. Timmer scratches my leg and does his hungry-face. I'm not leaving any for you—you've just had your biscuits, doggy-dog.

This is my sunny day and I'm going to sort things out. Even Mum is happy. She likes pottering round the house.

The shadows crackle as I pass the shed. Not today, not today—Mum said she'd take me to the doctor's if I don't stop doing the Backwards. I take a deep breath. Come on, Timmer. Let's go find that farm-man.

Cackler is leaning on the gatepost smoking his pipe as I walk up to his farm. I know he's the farmer because he shouted at me once for letting Timmer get too close to his cows. I've never spoken to him properly though. Up close, he's the wrinkliest man I've ever seen. His skin is brown and crinkly like the skin of a tree. He's as still as a tree too. He doesn't move, even when I'm standing next to him.

'Hello.' I don't know why but I don't mind talking to him. Normally I don't say anything to new people for ages.

Cackler takes a big puff from his pipe. Hidden in all the wrinkles, he's got dark brown eyes. They are all twinkly. He talks to me with the pipe still stuck in his mouth.

'You're Mikey, aren't you?'

'Yes, Mr . . . Mr . . . Cackler.' I'm trying to be polite but that sounds wrong.

The farmer lets out a low laugh. 'That's a bit formal! Most people just call me Cackler.' It's true—that's what everyone says. His eyes smile as if I just told a really good joke.

I smile extra-hard back at him.

He waves his pipe at Timmer. 'I recognize your dog.'

I nudge Timmer with my knee and he sits down. 'We haven't bothered your cows since last time.'

'Aye.' Cackler takes another puff and waves his pipe towards the river behind me. 'You found the tramp with Ralph, didn't you?'

I don't want to look at the river today. 'Yes. I found the tramp with your farm-man. Is that Ralph?'

Cackler nods. His eyes are kind. 'Death is a hard thing to see. Especially when it's out of its natural time.' He smiles. 'Mind you, birth is painful too. Changes, coming and going, that's the hard part.' He takes another puff.

Cackler makes me feel very quiet and still—Timmer too, I can tell. He blows a smoke ring. Round as round can be. Perfect. I like circles.

'Can I see him? Ralph, I mean?'

Cackler pulls the pipe from his mouth and dragon-smoke comes down his nose. He shakes his head. 'Sorry, he's not at work today.'

'It's just you and me today, isn't it, Gramps?' A curly-haired girl walks up behind Cackler without me seeing. She's sort of pretty with freckles and a big smile. I like freckles because the sun calls them up out of your skin. She's holding a bucket and puts it down on the gravel so she can put her hands on her hips. 'I wish it was just us *every* day.'

Cackler turns round and laughs. 'Ah, but Ralph gets a lot done when he's here.' Cackler looks back at me but I can't stop staring at the girl. 'Not too many people want to work on farms these days, do they, Mikey?'

'Eh?' I make a funny grunt.

The girl and Cackler laugh. Timmer wags his tail as he walks up to the girl.

'Oh, isn't he sweet!' The girl bends down to stroke him. 'I wish I was allowed a dog.'

I can see down her top. Cackler is watching me so I look the other way and go a bit red and shift from one foot to the other.

'Mum won't let me have any animals so I come to the farm whenever I can. Don't I, Gramps?'

'Aye.' Cackler smiles.

'What's he called?' The girl looks up at me.

'Timmer.'

Timmer makes his happy-snuffle noises and does a doggy-twirl just to show off. She laughs and rubs under his chin. 'You're cute, aren't you?'

'This is my granddaughter, Meg.' Cackler has his pipe back in his mouth and his eyes are extra-twinkly. 'She's a little wonder around the place.'

'Hi.' My face is hot. I rub the heel of my trainer into the gravel.

Meg smiles straight into my eyes with her green ones.

'I was *saying*, young Mikey, that not many people want to work on farms these days.' Cackler leans back against the fence post.

I follow where he's looking—at the fields and the trees and the cows and the space.

'I would,' I say.

Meg smiles and Cackler's pipe smoke floats up up up into the sky.

'Why don't you come and help me for a while, then? Old Mary is going to give birth soon—want to come and check on her with me?'

There's a load of sun in my head when he says that. Cackler wants me, me!, to help on the farm. I smile so hard my cheeks ache and I want to dance but I can't so I bend my knees a bit instead. Cackler laughs and shakes his head.

'Come on in then. But you better leave Timmer behind.'

Meg swings the gate open.

'Old Mary's up in this field.' Cackler points his pipe to the field that goes up the hill behind the farmhouse. 'This way.'

I snap the lead on Timmer and wind it round the gate-post. He looks at me with his head on one side. It's OK, Timmer-dog, it's not for long.

'Old Mary's a cow?' I run to keep up with Cackler.

He nods but doesn't stop. He walks really quickly for an old man. I turn back to look at Meg. She picks up her bucket again.

'Hurry up or he'll be gone. I've got to sort this out.'

She walks towards the barns at the other end of the farmyard. Then I remember my manners.

'Want some help?' I call.

'Nah! I'll manage. See you up there.'

I've never been in the cow-field behind the farmhouse before. The cows look up at us as we walk by. They don't stop eating the grass or move away. It's just like we're one of the herd too. I hop over the dung. It's all over the place. The cows really trample around and make it muddy too. Cackler doesn't say anything. He's getting faster and I almost have to run to keep up. His eyes keep looking just beyond the oak tree.

'Old Mary's all the way out here?'

He nods. 'She gave birth to her last two calves in the same place—just made her way to the old oak tree there and got on with it. Like to leave her where she's relaxed these days. Won't need much help.' He points at a calf near the hedge. 'That one was born a few weeks ago. Bess is her mum. We decided to leave them together a while. Now where is she?' He turns round slowly, then points to a thin cow up the hill a bit. 'That one. Hey, Bess, keep an eye on this little one will you?' Bess blinks her brown eyes and keeps chewing. 'Now where is Old Mary?'

She is lying down on the grass the other side of the old oak tree. There's a little dip in the ground and she's on her side. She's a funny shape—her sides have sort of gone in at the front a bit and her belly at the back is massive. She's straining, pushing. Her eyes are wide. Even though Cackler said she's done this lots of times before, I still think she's scared. I bet it hurts. I shiver but I'm not cold. Old Mary shivers too.

I walk closer to her head. There are flies on her nose. Cackler gives a low whistle. He shakes his head. 'Stay there, Mikey!' he says. 'Don't bother the old girl. She needs space.'

I stand still. Something funny is happening to me. I can feel the Backwards swirls but it feels different. Here in the middle of the field, the Backwards is pulling at me but it's lighter and it's softer. I breathe out slowly.

Old Mary lets out a loud cry. Her old body clenches

like a fist. She tries to scrabble up with her front legs. Cackler frowns, takes his hat off and wipes his head. All around me the soft Backwards is pulling at my head.

'Easy, girl, easy, girl.' Cackler leans over Old Mary but he doesn't touch her. He looks up at me with his brown eyes. He chews his lip. The quiet of the soft Backwards presses in my head and I squat down.

Old Mary cries again and tries to stand but she can't. She flicks her tail and her ears push back. The whites of her eyes flash. She's really frightened now. She tries to stand up again but she can't. Her body strains. Old Mary bellows. She's frightened and I hate it.

'This is the last time, old girl,' Cackler croons under his breath. 'Maybe it wasn't right to let you calf again, old lady.'

He moves towards her but she kicks out with her back legs. Cackler only just moves away in time. Some of the herd cry out too.

'Steady now, girl. Steady. Down again, Old Mary. Down like you usually do.' Cackler sings to her but her front legs keep scrabbling. 'You've got to settle, Old Mary. You've got to settle . . . '

I close my eyes. I let out a deep breath. This soft Backwards feels good. Like a warm bath. I've never felt it like this before. Old Mary scrabbles again. I want to help her. Cackler said that births, the comings and the goings, are the hardest. What if this Backwards could make things better, Old Mary? Shall I try?

I let it come. In my head all I can see is sunshine. Warm new sunshine. A warm wind blows. It's all right, Old Mary. I'm here now. Mikey will help you if he can.

I open my eyes.

There's a Backwards calf lying on the grass by Old Mary's head. It can't stand up yet. It is new and wet and wobbly.

Old Mary goes still; she stops trying to get up. It's one of her calves from long ago. Old Mary can see it—she's remembering.

The Backwards calf lies quiet. It's waiting until it's strong enough to stand. It kicks its brand new legs against the earth but it's still too weak to get up.

Old Mary's eyes calm down. She looks at her Backwards baby, sinks to the ground and pushes her nose towards it. She tries to lick it.

'That's it,' calls Cackler from the back, 'easy does it, Old Mary. Calm is good. You're OK girl, you're OK.' He stands up and looks straight at me. 'You calmed her right down, Mikey. Well done, lad!'

I helped! I helped Old Mary! Cackler saw it too! Mum said the Backwards was just in my head but it wasn't. It was here, today, and it was good. I wrap my arms round me tight and smile back at him.

Old Mary grunts. I look down. The Backwards calf is fading. It can't stay. Not today. The warm wind belongs around the new calf that's going to be born soon. Old Mary lets out a sigh and pushes again.

'Come here, Mikey!' Cackler is smiling. 'I can see the hooves!'

Meg is standing next to Cackler. I didn't hear her arrive. Her eyes are shining.

'I love this bit,' she whispers.

I can't answer because of the sunshine in my head. I wish Timmer was here to see this. I don't know why, but I wish Mum was here too.

'Can you see them?' whispers Meg.

There's a yellowy bag thing hanging out of the cow but that can't be right, can it?

'See what?'

As soon as I've said it, I get what she means. Two white things are coming out the back of Old Mary. Cackler is holding up the tail out the way. I giggle—shit and babies all coming out the back of Old Mary. She bellows and strains again. I stop laughing.

I can start to see the legs. The calf is coming out feet first and the white things are little hooves. I crouch down. Meg taps me on the shoulder. I smile but I don't look at her. All the world is waiting, holding its breath. If we speak, the quiet'll smash to bits.

The head is coming now. I can see it. The calf is all wrapped up in a bag. Its eyes are closed and it's pressing against the sack-thing like it's too tight. This is the first time—the very first time—it is in the world. Another push and the body slips out, quick like a slippery fish. The sack rips round the calf's head. It's wet and new new new. Cackler breathes out a sigh.

'Good girl, Old Mary, good girl.'

He grabs the calf by the legs, still all squishy in the bag, and drags it round to Old Mary's head. I follow. I want to see this. I crouch down straight away. The warm wind is strong.

For a minute they don't do anything. Old Mary looks down. She's tired. The calf is still. I can hear a blackbird singing in the oak tree. The long grass whispers.

The calf twitches, struggles to move. **The Backwards is gentle around it; the calf is so new that its Backwards hasn't got a shape yet—it's just like clear water at the edge of a lake, lapping around it. Everything is sparkly.** Old Mary leans over, her long pink tongue starts to lick the sack from her baby. The calf is still for a moment. The warm wind is everywhere.

'Look!' Meg holds my arm. 'Mum and her baby!'

Cackler nods. 'What d'you think then, Mikey?'

I look down at my arm. Meg's hand is brown with golden hairs on it. It makes me tingle. Old Mary keeps licking the calf.

''S brilliant,' I whisper. 'Just brilliant.'

The calf is already starting to move. It can't get up yet but it's trying. Old Mary strokes it with her tongue. Meg takes her hand away. My arm feels cold.

Cackler puts his hands on his hips. 'This calf'll be her

last . . . ' He bends down. 'What say we leave this one with you, in the field?' He reaches out and pats Old Mary on the head. 'Eh?'

'What? Where else would the calf go?' I wrinkle my nose.

'Usually, Gramps takes the calves away from their mother two days after they are born,' Meg says. 'It's kinder to take them away quickly because then the bond isn't too strong.'

Old Mary's calf tries to stand on its brand new thin legs. Wobbles but nearly there.

'Why?'

Meg laughs. 'So we take the milk, of course!'

'We drink the milk that's supposed to be for the calf?' Is that *right*?

'Yes, lad! You townies!' Cackler's eyes twinkle at me. 'But I've made my mind up. Old Mary's old—will be better for both of 'em if they stay together a while.'

The calf pushes hard and is on its feet. Will you look at that! On its feet and it's only just been born! I let out a whoop.

'Woooooooooooo hoooooooooooo!'

The blackbird flies out of the tree. The little calf falls down. Far away, I hear Timmer yowling back to me. Cackler frowns.

'Settle down, young Mikey. Maybe best if you leave these two now . . . '

I don't want to go. I smile goodbye to the calf and Old Mary and Cackler and Meg.

'Come back soon, Mikey!' Meg calls to me as I go.

The warm wind whispers around me as I walk down the field back to the farmyard. What a cool day! Cackler let me onto his farm. I saw a baby calf born. The Backwards was good. A girl put her hand on my arm and I can still feel it, warm and tingly, even now it's gone.

Chapter Eight

There's a note on the table when I get home. I wanted to tell Mum about everything but I can't because she's not here.

Gone to the police. Don't worry. Back soon. Mum xxx

I sit for a while. I understand this note. It took me a while to get the 'police' bit but Mum always says nearly the same thing in her notes so I get what she's saying. 'Gone to the shops. Don't worry. Back soon. Mum xxx.' Or 'Gone to the hairdresser's. Don't worry. Back soon. Mum xxx.' I don't know why she would go to the police. Maybe she forgot to tell the black-and-whites something but she says 'Don't worry' so that means that it's all right. Mum didn't put that once and I went a bit mad and Albert from next door had to come and sit next to me to keep me still and quiet until she got back so she always remembers to say that now. 'Don't worry.'

I make myself a cheese'n'onion crisp sandwich and roll it nice and flat with a rolling-pin and then I go and sit in the garden with Timmer. I am still all fizzy inside. I can't believe today. I want to tell someone but Albert and Gavin'n'Tina aren't in their gardens. I walk up the street and back again but still Mum isn't back.

Timmer and me end up sitting watching TV for ages—until it gets dark outside which is late in the summer—and then we've had enough so we go to bed.

Behind the curtains, out in the garden, the shadows in the shed are getting louder, hissing. Timmer snuffles my hand to tell me it's OK. Maybe it's because I'm worried because Mum isn't back yet. Do you think that's it, doggy-dog? He looks at me with his brown eyes, head on one side. We both know that's not quite right. It's something else, too.

I lie, waiting. Timmer is on the floor. My head is all jumbled with the tramp and Dad and new calves and Meg. The world has gone funny and lots of new things are muddling up—very good things and very bad things, all together. Normally I go into the shed when I get muddled like this, but I can't because there's something bad in there. I pull my knees up to my chin so I'm as small as I can be. I don't know. I scrunch my face up to see if I can think any better but I can't. I hate my scar sometimes.

Chapter Eight

A key turns in the lock. Mum's home at last! She clicks the landing light on as she comes upstairs. I wait for her to look into my room to say goodnight but her feet keep walking past my door and she goes straight into her own bedroom.

I sit up. That's not like her.

I hear her talking. She must be on the phone in her room. Her voice is cracked. She's crying. She's not all right. I swing my legs out of bed and rub my toes against Timmer's head. He grunts. I tiptoe over to my bedroom door and open it. Mum's door is nearly closed. I can see the edge of her—her back—as she talks on the phone. Her head is all hunched over so I can only see a little bit of her new red hair sticking up.

'Can't believe it.' Her voice has rips in it like it's falling to bits. 'And I've only just found out. The bastards.'

I take a step closer. It doesn't feel right to go in and talk to her. I don't think she wants me to see her.

'And how can I tell . . . Mikey . . .' Her words are falling apart—flying away—she blows her nose. I have to step nearer to hear her when she starts talking again. I don't make a sound.

'But . . . I've always told him that his father has gone . . . gone . . . and so . . . ' Mum stops so her words will come back. She is very still. I am too. Even Timmer doesn't move from my bedroom door, waiting for Mum to finish.

Her voice is quieter than a whisper when she speaks.

'Why did he do it? Why would he . . . ' Her shoulders shake. What has Dad done? What? What? What?

Mum leans over towards her knees. I see her hands so tight on the red phone that the knobbly bits are white.

'But I can never tell Mikey what he did—never—never . . . ' She lets out a sob like the world is ending.

'Never.'

The light on the landing suddenly pops and goes out. I hold my breath. Mum's head turns a little bit but she doesn't stand up. She's almost a shadow now—her face is lit by her bedside light but I can't see it from here. I check behind me. The funny bumpy wallpaper has extra-long shadows and it's black down the stairs. I shiver.

What has Dad done? What will she never tell me?

I want Timmer. I go back into my room and sit on my bed. I don't even have to tell him to jump up because he's already there and I can put my arms round his neck and hide my face. His fur is rough and curly. The world is breaking up into tiny pieces like smashed glass and I can't put them back together. I can't work the jigsaw out. My head hurts and I have to close my eyes. I push my fingers into Timmer's fur so hard that he whines but he doesn't pull away from me.

I am so stupid Mum won't tell me what's happened.

Dad has done something so wrong that we can't talk about it.

The tramp is dead and I don't know why.

But Old Mary had a calf today. I helped. I was there. Cackler was there. Meg was there with her freckles and green eyes. Timmer licks my face. Let's go back tomorrow to find the farm man, Ralph. Maybe he knows what happened to the tramp.

I'm up first. Mum's bedroom door is shut tight. She usually leaves it open. I stand outside and lean on one foot then the other. The floor creaks. I keep lifting my hand to knock on the door but what if she's asleep? What if she's tired? What if she doesn't want to see me like she didn't last night?

I sit on the floor. My belly rumbles. I'm hungry. I want breakfast.

Then I have the best idea ever. I'm so excited I hug Timmer so hard he yelps. Shhhhhh, Timmer! Be quiet! Come downstairs. Help me make the surprise. Mum was sad last night so I'm going to cheer her up and make breakfast for her!

I do a little dance down the stairs. Breakfast for Mum! Breakfast for Mum! Coffee first. I put water in the kettle. I press the red button like Mum taught me. I do a little jig! I'm going to make Mum's eyes shine, Timmer! I'll make it better like I did for Old Mary! I switch the radio on. I want some music like we have at school when we cook. Mum doesn't like listening to music any more but I think she's just forgotten how nice it is. I find some jazz stuff, I bend my legs and whizz round in a spin.

I open the cupboard. Beans. Beans on toast. I open the can. It takes a while but I do it without cutting myself. That's good, Mikey. Very good. I put the beans in the saucepan and turn on the gas ring. Low, Mikey—that's what the cookery teacher says. Keep it low.

Bread in the toaster—ping! Milk. Mum likes hot milk in coffee. I pour some into a saucepan on another ring on the hob. Look at that, Timmer! Two rings on the hob! I'm a proper chef. I need one of those big white hats! I stick my finger into the beans. They're not very hot. I stir them but they're still cold. The toast will be ready in a minute. I whack up the knob so the blue flame is nice and big. I rub my hands.

The sun is shining and Mum's going to be so chuffed!

Timmer is in the garden, watching me. He's dropped the tennis ball in front of him. He barks. He wants to play. I go outside. It's so quiet. No one else is up, not even Albert. Timmer's mouth is open, tongue hanging out. His eyes follow me everywhere. I pick up the ball. I pretend to throw it towards the shed to put him off, but Timmer isn't fooled. He barks again. I throw it hard down the garden. Timmer's off before the ball even leaves my hand. He knows just where it'll land. The new sun shines on his scruffy coat as he runs. He's back, soggy ball dropped right next to my feet. He crouches, ears forward. *Again, Mikey, again.*

I throw it towards the apple tree this time. The grass underneath is still wet and covered with spiders' webs, bobbly with water drops. Timmer smashes through them and he's back. The garden is too little for Timmer really. When we go to the beach, he can run and run and run as far as he likes. I'm going to take the tennis racket so I can hit the ball miles away. I'll hit it into the sea too so he gets wet. He'll love it. He's never been to the sea before.

'WHAT'S GOING ON?' Mum is in the kitchen and she's shouting.

I rush back inside. There's smoke coming out the bean saucepan and the milk is bubbling out the other one. Mum's hair is everywhere. Her face is white-white-white with red eyes. She throws the bean pan in the sink. Turns off the knobs. Turns off the radio. Sits at the table with her head in her hands. She's shaking. I knit my fingers together and hop from one foot to the other.

'I was making breakfast as a surprise . . . '

Mum looks up, her mouth is pushed together. 'Ah, but you WEREN'T were you, Mikey? You were down the bloody garden with the bloody dog leaving me to clear up the bloody mess—same as everyone! Same as EVERY-ONE!' She puts her head back between her hands. 'How many times have you been told not to use the cooker un-less a grown-up is here. Hey?'

I rub one shoe up the back of the other leg. Lots of times. I forgot. I was just trying to help. What can I say to make her better, Timmer? What will make her happy?

'Is it today we're going to the beach, Mum?'

Mum's hands drop to the table. She stares at me, mouth open.

'You've got a cheek! No we are NOT going to the beach. Can't you see I'm upset? Don't you know how much I have to do on my own?' Her mouth wobbles. She starts to cry.

I go to her but she holds up her hands.

'Just go, Mikey! Just leave me alone! Give me some peace! And take that mutt with you!'

I walk fast fast fast down the garden. I stop when I get to the shed. The shadows are shrieking but I don't care. Now we're not going to be happy and smiling on the beach! Look how upset Mum is! I kick the side of the shed hard hard HARD so the door rattles.

I run as fast as I can, out into the fields back to Cackler's farm with Timmer barking beside me.

Chapter Nine

Ralph is standing behind the cows in the farmyard when I get there. He's making sure they all go out the gate and up into the fields and he's opened his arms wide to stop them turning back. Every now and then he stamps his feet to scare them. He doesn't need to. The cows are slow and gentle but they know what to do. There's a big bossy cow who is pushing from the side to get through the gate first—I think she must be the leader of the cows. The Bossy Boots.

I reckon Ralph's been milking them in the big barn. I can smell it.

'Move along, girls.' He turns round and sees me. He winks. 'Moooooove along.'

I don't wink back. I can't. They laugh at me at school because I shut both eyes at the same time. I can't just close one. I smile instead.

Once he's shut the gate behind the cows and they're safe in the field, he walks over to me. He's wearing a T-shirt with long sleeves today so I can't see the picture of the naked lady on his arm. He's all sweaty. His face is a bit white and wrinkly though like he hasn't had enough sleep.

'You're the lad from the river, en't yer?'

I nod. I smile again. I want him to like me.

'Bit of a shock, that, eh?' He rubs his hair with his hands and then leans against the fence and picks at a bit of wood on it. 'Sorry for calling the police about yer, mate.' The man looks up at me and then back to the fence. He pulls a strip of wood right off so the white wood underneath shows.

I am starting to panic a bit now. I remember to smile. I don't know what to say when he talks about the black-and-whites but Mum said it was all right, didn't she? She made it all right, didn't she?

'It's just it was all a shock, you know, finding the body,' he digs his nail into the white soft bit of wood, 'and you said you knew the tramp's body was there but I didn't know how you knew.'

He waits. I don't know what to say. I can't talk about the Backwards to him. Mum said so. My stomach is all hard and swirly at the same time. I don't know what to do. I pull the hair at the back of my head so hard that it hurts. Stupid Mikey, stupid Mikey.

The farm-man looks up at me and goes quiet and then says, 'But it's all sorted now, hey?'

I nod. I take a deep breath.

'I'm not a bad 'un.'

'No, mate, no, course not!' He pats my shoulder over the fence and goes a bit red and when I catch his eye he looks away quick. I think he feels bad, Timmer. Hey, did you hear what I said, Timmer? He feels bad because he told the black-and-whites about me.

He doesn't think I'm a bad 'un.

He swings the gate open and holds out his arm to shake my hand.

'I'm Ralph, mate.'

'Hello.' I squeeze his hand and then I do what Mum hates before thinking about it and I pat him on the top of his arm. A double pat; one, two.

Ralph has a funny look on his face when I do that. He rubs his hands down his shirt and watches me ever so closely.

'Did the black-and-whites find out who killed the tramp?' I scrunch up my nose. I don't like talking about the tramp but I want to know.

'Not yet, mate. They're still working on it I suppose.' Ralph nods down towards Timmer. 'You like animals, don't yer?'

I push Timmer with my knee to say hello but he sits down hard and won't move. I nudge him again but he looks the other way.

'Yes.'

'You're always with that dog and you like fishing and you knew 'bout the bittern . . . '

I nod. I did tell him that.

Ralph smiles at me. 'Fancy coming in here and having a look round? We've got quite a few animals.'

'Yeah!'

'Come on then, Mikey. Pigs first.'

This is brilliant. I tie Timmer up like last time and follow Ralph. I look round for Meg and Cackler but I can't see anyone.

'Is anyone else here today?'

'At market, mate.' Ralph winks at me again. 'While the cat's away . . . '

'He took the cat?'

'No, mate!' Ralph laughs at me but I don't know why.

The pigs—there are eight of them—live in the little field to the back of the house. You have to feed them once a day and they are massive but if you fed them eight times a day they would just keep on eating and eating.

'If they're really stressed, pigs will even eat their own babies,' Ralph says, rubbing the back of his neck and arching his back.

That makes me quiet. I watch them. They're happy. I can't imagine them doing anything bad like that. If you look the biggest one in the eye, you can tell that she's clever. She's like an old lady with white thick hairs sticking out of her skin. She knows all sorts of secrets, I can tell. If I was on my own with her, I'd let her Backwards come but there isn't time now. I can feel it a little bit anyway—it's quiet and deep and goes down into the earth like roots.

'C'mon, Mikey.' Ralph takes me by the arm and we're off again.

We say hello to the cows as we walk along the edge of their field to the next barn but we don't go in the field. The sun is hot hot hot on my head. Bossy Boots cow is standing under a tree, watching me. I look for Bess and Old Mary and their calves but they were over in the next field along and I can't see them from here. Then we go inside the barn. It's cooler in here.

Oh, look! Look at that! There's a row of little heads sticking out the side of the pen in the barn. Calves. One, two, three, four, five, six, seven, eight of them. They're eating some straw stuff on the ground outside their pen.

'Four months old, these little 'uns.' Ralph reaches out and scratches one of them on the head between the eyes.

The calves are brown and white but they are so white-white that you can tell they are brand new. Pink noses. Pink tongues. I copy him and reach out to the littlest calf. It doesn't move. It looks scared though and then it takes a step away from me.

'That one's not well.' Ralph nods at my calf.

'What's wrong with it?' I take my hand away and the calf moves forward towards the straw again and takes a bite.

'A stomach upset thing. Unless it's going to infect the other calves, it's always best to keep 'em together. Take a sick calf away from his pals and he gets really upset.'

I nod. I understand that.

'Makes 'em even more ill sometimes when you separate 'em.'

I bend down and look my sick calf in the eye. 'Will it get better?'

'Oh yeah. Should think so.'

I want to sit quietly next to the little calf but Ralph starts stamping up and down alongside the pens. Shhh, Ralph! The calves don't like it—they back away from him a little. He claps his hands and they jump. He laughs.

'Silly critters. Ready to go then, Mikey?'

He leads me over to the chickens next. Down the orchard, past the big trough, and round the old tractor, they live in a coop. Lots of them. Feathers on the ground. Jerky heads as they peck at the food. They ignore me. Their feathers are shiny though. That means they are nice and healthy.

As Ralph walks me back to the gate, I wish I could go and sit with the pigs and the calves again. I would be so still that they wouldn't mind me being there at all. I might even make the calf feel better like I did Old Mary. When I get home I'm going to tell Mum that I know what I want to be when I get older. People ask me and I don't know but now I do. I want to be a farmer, like Cackler. I like him.

We're back in the farmyard now, and Ralph goes into a little outhouse next to Cackler's house while I untie Timmer. There's a fridge in there and he brings out two beers. Timmer is pulling me towards the gate but I stop and wait for Ralph.

'Want one? It's another scorcher. I'm parched.'

I nod. He hands me the beer. Me! A beer! I smile and try to pretend that I do this all the time but I can't stop my legs jiggling. We lean against the fence, him and me. Ralph and me. My mate Ralph.

'I just realized who you remind me of.'

'Who?'

He's looking at me out the corner of his eye. He looks a bit serious. I feel something tighten in my stomach. Have I done something wrong?

'Yeah. It was when you patted me on the shoulder after you shook my hand.' He takes a long swig of beer and looks up at the top of the hill. 'You're Stu Baxter's son, aren't you?'

There's a far away screech in my head. I'm in the middle of drinking some beer and it goes down the wrong way—I cough and it comes down my nose. How does he know that? How does he know about Dad? I look at Ralph but he keeps staring up at the hill. I wipe my nose on my sleeve. I don't know what to say. Mum's going to kill me. I'm not supposed to . . . I'm not supposed to talk about . . .

Ralph takes another swig of beer.

'It's OK, mate. It's OK.'

My head is swirling and I don't want it to. What does he know about Dad? How does he know about Dad?

'Just bad luck, he had, that's all,' says Ralph.

Bad luck?

'I knew him a bit. You know, before, like.'

Ralph turns round and looks at me. My head is starting to hurt. He's got this look on his face I don't understand. My hands are going slippy on the bottle of beer.

'You hear much from him?'

I shake my head.

'Nah, I don't suppose . . . ' He grins. 'Well, if you do, mate, tell him Ralph sends his best.'

I don't nod. I don't know what to do. I never hear from Dad apart from in the shed. But Ralph is my mate. My new mate. I feel woozy. Timmer is still pulling me away from the farm and won't sit down—when I push his bum to the floor with my knee, he growls like thunder. Ralph picks at the label on the bottle of beer. His face goes tight but he smiles when he looks at me.

'He was up for games, was yer dad.' He takes a swig. 'Fun and games, mate.'

Mum said Dad's fun was dangerous and that's how he landed in prison. I feel the line of the scar down my head—it's aching. I see Dad's bruised face in the shed. I see the chisel. I wrap my arms around me tight.

'You OK?'

Ralph is looking at me with that funny look on his face again. The world is swirly but I want Ralph to be my mate.

I nod and take a swig of beer. It tastes of the shed. The shadows in the grass are waking up.

'Cool. Like father, like son?'

He's watching me—looking straight at me. I look back for a second. What's the right answer? What does he want me to say? I don't know, I don't know, I don't know.

I smile.

'Good lad.' Ralph slaps me on the arm. 'Good lad! Fancy joining me later for a beer and we can chat?'

He's smiling at me, Timmer! He wants to meet for a beer. I did the right thing.

'Yeah!'

'Horse and Hounds after eight then?'

'Yeah!'

As I start to walk back up the path away from the farm, Timmer races ahead chasing smells. He can't get away fast enough. It doesn't matter that I can't get into the shed tonight because I'm going out with Ralph. What if the others from the normal school are there and they see me? See me, having a beer with my mate Ralph! My head is singing and singing. A beer with Ralph. The shadows are starting to laugh but I just sing even louder so I can't hear them.

Chapter Ten

My feet go heavy as I get near home. I'd forgotten about the row with Mum this morning. My breakfast mess. The crying. I stop at the top of the garden. I twist the bottom of my T-shirt. I don't want to go in.

Albert is in his garden watering his plants, long blue ones. His white hair looks like a cloud on top of his head.

'How are you, Mikey? Fine day, isn't it?'

'Yes.'

He's always smiling when he's in his garden, is Albert. Even when it's raining. I look up at our kitchen window but I can't see Mum.

'How's your mother, Mikey?' Albert watches me as he squirts water at his flowers.

'Not good, Albert. She was really cross this morning cos I messed up making breakfast.'

'Oh dear. I'm sure you were doing your best.'

He smiles. I don't. It wasn't all right. It wasn't all right at all. Albert rubs his nose, then reaches out and snaps off some of the long blue flowers. One, two, three, four, five. 'Here you go. Your mum mentioned the other day that she likes these.' He hands them over the fence to me. 'Flowers and upset women—good combination, lad. Useful lesson to last a lifetime.'

I smile a thank you. The flowers are beautiful. I hold them up near my face so the petals stroke my chin. They are butterfly-wing-soft.

But when I walk into the kitchen, Mum isn't there. Pat is sitting at the kitchen table, squashed out over two chairs. As soon as she sees me, her mouth stretches into a not-real smile. Something is wrong.

'Hello there!' Her face is full of colours. Blue eyes. Red cheeks. Pink lips. Makes me woozy. 'Your mum's not feeling well—gone to Gran's for a couple of days, so I've come to stay.' She squeezes her cheeks into another pretend smile.

'What's wrong with her? It's me, isn't it? It's me being bad this morning?' I twist the T-shirt again.

'Ohhh, Mikey, *of course* it's not you! She's just had a lot on her plate. Batteries run low.' She holds out her arms; the skin underneath them swings. 'Come here, sweetheart!'

She puffs as she stands up. Pat can't hug me properly any more—she's too small and her head only goes up to my armpits but she smells of flowery stuff, just the way she always smells, and she's squishy like hugging a cushion. My shoulders drop and I rest my chin on the top of her head. I want to cry.

'Don't worry. Don't worry.' She pats my back. 'It'll all be better soon. Hey, what's this?' She pulls away. 'Oh! We're squashing these lovely flowers!'

'They were for Mum.'

'You *are* sweet, Mikey! Let me sort them out.' She goes bustly and puts them in a pink spotty vase on the windowsill, stands back to look at them. 'Everything will be all right. You'll see. Your mum just needs a bit of time, that's all.'

I sit down. 'She's not mad at me?'

'Nooooooo!' Pat shakes her head and smiles at me, then goes back to the vase and fiddles around so the flower-faces are looking at us. 'Now don't they look a picture?'

I don't care about the bloody flowers! I care about Mum. My head starts to hurt. What's wrong with her? What? I put the empty coffee cups on the table in a neat line.

'It's Dad isn't it?'

Pat goes really still.

'She came home last night and she was crying down the phone about him.'

Pat turns round—it's the not-real smile again. 'Oh Mikey, you know she's always upset about your dad.

I know!' The smile stretches up to her ears. 'Let's text her a picture of these flowers to cheer her up!' She pulls out her mobile phone. 'Shall we say "Get well soon! Love Mikey"? Then you can phone tomorrow when she's had a good night's sleep. OK?'

I nod. Mum will like that. 'Will she be back soon?'

'Oh a day or two and I'm sure she'll be on the mend. *We* can have fun though, can't we? Maybe a pizza and film tonight?'

Then I remember. 'I can't.' I puff out my chest. 'I'm going out with a friend, Pat.'

Her eyebrows go up so the blue above her eyes gets bigger. 'Who, Mikey?'

'Someone I met at Cackler's farm.' I smile. 'A *mate*.'

'A new friend, hey?' Pat makes an ooooo-shape with her mouth. 'He's a nice man, Cackler. You could do with some fun. I'll wait up for you, mind. Until you're back home safely.'

I scuffle my feet together under the table. I like Pat but I don't want her to wait up for me. I swallow hard. I want it to be Mum.

I get to the pub early. The sun is soft and is going down behind the hills. It's a red sky—that means it'll be another hot day tomorrow. There are some people sitting in the pub garden but I don't want them to look at me so I keep my head down. I walk with Timmer past the gate to the pub garden up towards the next street and then walk back again. I don't know what to do.

'Hey, Mikey!'

It's Toby and Dave and Jim. They're sitting at a wooden bench-table-thing in the pub garden. They are right at the edge, away from everyone else. Timmer growls and steps close to me. I put my hand on his collar. He's been in a bad mood ever since we left home. We are on our best behaviour today, Timmer. Ralph will be here soon.

He growls again.

'Fancy a drink, Mikey?' Dave shouts and he holds his hands to his eyes to shade them from the setting sun. 'Don't be a boring bastard. Come and join us.'

Jim says something quietly and then snorts into his pint of beer, his red curly hair blowing in the breeze. Toby hits the table as he laughs and waves me over.

'Come over here, Mikey!'

I start to move and then stop because everyone will stare at me as I walk by. Jim puffs on his fag, holds my eye and then pats the seat next to him.

D'you see that, Timmer? They want me to join them—even Jim and he's the leader of the pack. Me, with them! They are loads older than me and they want me to go over. We've got to look cool, Timmer. This is our lucky day.

Timmer sits down by the gate and won't move. Why

are you doing this? Stop it! You're embarrassing me. I push Timmer hard with my knee but he still won't move so I have to clip his lead on and drag him over to the table. He whimpers. Don't let me down, Timmer, not today. This is important.

I sit next to Jim. His eyes look a bit blurry like Mum's do sometimes. He claps his hands and bows his head like I have just made Timmer do a good trick. Timmer lies down, slumps his head on his paws and looks the other way.

'Good lad, good lad.' Dave rubs his hands together and stands up—he never keeps still. 'My treat, mate. I'll get you a pint. No one will see you out here with us.' He taps the side of his nose as he walks back to the bar.

'So, Mikey-Mikey,' Toby leans over, 'had any more of your funny turns recently?' He drums his fingers on the table. His nails are bitten right down and they are bleeding a bit. He looks over at Jim. Jim laughs and draws on his fag.

'No.' I shake my head. I've been fine for ages now. Mostly. Far away, I can hear a whisper of the shadows in my head but it's a long way away. I make my fingers go stiff to make myself ignore it. Jim laughs again.

'What you doing here at this pub on your own? Won't serve a boy, now, will they?' Jim's face is close to mine and his breath smells bad.

I shake my head.

'Soooooooooooo . . . ?' He puts his head on one side. 'What you up to?'

'Meeting a friend.' There's a fizzy happy feeling in my throat when I say that. My mate, Ralph. My mate. Toby snorts and drains his glass.

'A real friend or an imaginary one, Mikey?'

Jim leans close to me. I feel a bit panicky because I don't know what he means but he's smiling at me, so it must be good. I smile back. Jim throws back his head and laughs and I can see the pink of his mouth.

'Oi, drink up, drink up, lads.'

Dave is back. He is carrying four pints all squashed together and plonks them down onto the table. Some of the beer sloshes down the sides of the glasses. Four glasses. All the same size. I am drinking with the men today, Timmer.

Timmer?

He's still ignoring me.

'Down in one, hey, Mikey-Mikey?' Jim raises his glass at me.

'Yeah!' I'm one of the lads today.

They all cheer and I feel sunshine in my head and I drink and drink and drink as hard as I can. I see the others and they are pros; they've nearly finished. They are leaning back and I can see the gulps go down their necks. They remind me a bit of my bittern but her neck is much more beautiful. Beer dribbles down my chin. The bittern makes me want the quiet of the river. I can't breathe. I gulp some more but I feel like I'm drowning. My head is filling up with black. Something is stab stab stabbing me behind my eyes and burning my throat and rising up and up in my neck.

I have to stop. I put the glass down. It is only about half full.

The other three glasses are empty.

Jim looks over at me and shakes his head slowly. 'Tut, tut, Mikey.' Dave and Toby nudge each other.

I've let them down. I was supposed to join in—one of the lads—and I let them down.

'Sorry,' I whisper.

Dave laughs again and taps on the table. Jim holds his fag over the top of my glass and flicks ash into my beer. It floats on the top like drowned ants.

'Penalty, mate. Down the hatch.'

I watch him while I drink. They like me when I drink. They whoop and laugh and Jim slaps me on the back. It makes me forget the scratchy feeling of the fag ash on the back of my throat. My eyes sting and my head hurts but I won't, won't, won't stop until I've finished the pint. I'm out with the lads.

I slam the empty glass on the table.

I can hear a loud whistling wind in my head. The table looks like it's moving but it doesn't matter because I am one of them today.

I smile at Jim. He smiles back and his mouth twists a bit at the corners. He looks at Dave and Toby and then at me.

'Want to be part of our gang, Mikey?'

He reaches into his jacket pocket as he speaks.

Lightning flashes in my mind and cuts through the woozy feeling. I can sit out in pubs with them and the other lads at normal school will see me and they'll all like me. I nod hard even though it makes my head hurt.

'Need to pass a test then, mate.'

Dave and Toby laugh quietly. Jim has pulled out his hip flask. Firewater. He pours two fingers into the bottom of my pint glass. He looks at me, smiles and then tips all the stuff from the ashtray into it. A fag soup. Toby's eyes are watering and his shoulders are shaking. Dave frowns a little bit—he screws up his face and nearly says something, then stops. They all lean forwards—their tongues are hanging out like panting dogs. Jim slides the glass over to me.

'Bottoms up, Mikey,' he whispers.

I'm going to be one of their gang. Me, Mikey. They like me.

I lift up the glass. It smells awful. It smells like mornings after a big argument at home. Mum's red puffy eyes. Slamming doors. Cold chips for breakfast. Far away, I hear Dad singing in the shower. Something is stuck in my throat that makes my eyes sting. I don't know if this feels good.

'Down in one,' sings Jim softly, tapping the wooden table, 'down in one, down in one . . .'

They lean in close. I take a deep breath and lift the glass again. The firewater sludge is sliding down towards my mouth. My eyes are streaming and I want to gag. Timmer snarls at Jim and his teeth flash.

'Down in one, down in one . . .'

I feel something tearing in my head. I don't know if I like this.

'That'll do, lads!'

A loud voice cuts through the smell of the firewater and I look up.

It's Ralph.

My mate Ralph.

He's come for me. Mum has gone away but Ralph is here.

Jim and Dave and Toby sit back. Dave stands and tries to shake Ralph's hand but Ralph ignores him and snatches the glass from me.

'It was just a bit of fun, mate . . .' says Dave but Ralph flicks his hand at him and Dave stops talking.

Ralph lifts up my glass and swirls it round, a dark sludge, then tips it upside-down so the firewater sinks into the grass and the fag ash makes a little dark mound. Jim coughs and pulls another fag from his pocket. Ralph stares at them and shakes his head. We all look down at the fag ash. They wanted me to drink that to join their gang but Ralph stopped them. He rescued me. I smile at

Ralph as I sway; I can see two of him, maybe three. Ralph puts his hand on my elbow to pull me up from my seat and shakes his head again at the lads.

'Come on, Mikey.'

I stand up and the world twizzles. Where's Timmer? I turn to look for him. Dave is looking at me, watching me—I think he's almost sorry. Timmer is next to me. He looks at Ralph and then the lads—his ears are flat on the back of his head. I hold his lead tight.

Ralph chooses a table far away from everyone round the corner near the children's playground. As I follow him across the grass, the shadows start to whisper. My legs are wobbly and there is a funny whooshing in my head that makes me dizzy. Ralph goes off to the bar. I look around me—have I been to this pub garden before? Timmer whines and scratches the ground next to my feet.

Ralph comes back and pushes a pint of Coke across the table to me. 'You need to sober up a bit, Mikey.'

The Coke fizz tickles my throat.

Out of the corner of my eye, I see Little Mikey, arms out, running round the pub garden like an aeroplane. Zig zag. Round the tables and over the clouds.

I look over at Ralph to see if he can see Little Mikey too but Ralph is blurry. He's watching me and smiling because he's my mate but I can't see him properly. **I can't see anything properly now because Dad is here. He's sitting next to Ralph.**

Dad.

My Backwards dad.

He's watching Little Mikey. He's watching him like he's his special boy. Everything is melting. Dad is smiling.

Ralph has rescued me. I lean back on the bench and lift my feet off the floor so I'm just balancing on my bum. I'm floating. I'm crying.

Dad picks up his pint, takes a sip and then wipes his mouth on the back of his hand.

'We're mates, aren't we, Ralph?' My voice is far away.

Little Mikey whizzes behind me, blond curly hair flying. Dad is following him with his eyes all round the pub garden.

I feel dizzy with it all.

Ralph smiles. 'Sure, Mikey.' He balances the beer mat half on the table, half off, then flips it—quick like a snake—and catches it with his hand.

I hold my arms out. I'm still floating. **I want Dad to watch me but he can only see Little Mikey.** Ralph flips the beer mat again. I lean further back.

'Actually, as we're mates, can I ask you something?' Ralph looks up at me.

'Of course!' Did you hear that, Timmer? Ralph said 'as we're mates'!

'I need some help from time to time.' He grins at me. 'And I might have a job coming up that you could help me with. Would that be OK?'

He might have a job for me? For ME?!!!

Dad smiles across at Little Mikey.

Ralph raises his eyebrows. 'What do you reckon? Fancy doing that for your old mate Ralph?'

'Yeah!'

Ralph laughs, all gurgly in his throat. Timmer growls under the table. I had forgotten he was there. My mate Ralph has saved me from the lads and now we're going to do stuff together. I might even help him out! I lift my feet higher off the ground. I could float up and into the night sky and far away.

On the other side of the table, Little Mikey runs past Dad. He trips over and falls in slow motion.

I wobble as I watch him.

'Steady, Mikey.' Ralph looks over his beer. I hold my arms straight to balance and nearly fall. His eyes shine.

Dad is looking out for Little Mikey. One minute he was sitting drinking his pint, just watching. Then he's there and Little Mikey is caught, safe in his arms.

My head swirls and my eyes sting. I smile at Ralph. He toasts me with his glass. I nod and the world tilts . . . and tilts . . . and tilts . . .

My neck cracks as my head hits the ground. My legs are caught under the table-bench. The world is spinning.

Ralph leans over the table, but all I can see is his dark shape. He tuts at me. 'Time to get you home, mate.'

Little knives stab in my head. I can't stand because I am shaking but then Timmer is here—his tongue soft and warm on my cheek. Ralph shakes his head.

'C'mon, you oaf.' He walks out the pub garden, turning to see if I follow him.

Timmer keeps right next to me. The world is still topsy-whirly. I turn round slowly before I leave. I look hard even though my eyes are blurry but I can't see them any more.

Dad and Little Mikey have gone.

Chapter Eleven

Ralph looks out the car window to make sure I get inside the house safely. He revs the engine hard as I open the front door. The wheels screech as he drives up the street.

'Hey, your mum says thanks for the flowers!' Pat shouts from Mum's bedroom when I get in.

The house is wrong without Mum. Pat has been tidying up and my room is too straight. She's made it smell too sugary. The smells curl up my nose as I lie in bed and make me feel sick. The duvet makes me sweat but I don't have a sheet and I need something cosy. My head hurts. Everything is moving. Nothing will stay still. I make Timmer stay close even though it's hot.

All night my scar aches. The tramp laughs in my dreams. Dad walks round and round the shed, waiting for me. My head is all tangled-string when the sun gets up.

I go downstairs and pour a glass of milk and sit at the kitchen table. It's early, I can tell by the light. It's brand new ready for a brand new day. My eyes hurt so I have to squint when I look out the window. There's a wind in the apple tree and the leaves are whispering. The shed is dark. I think I see the door move, but then it's still. The shadows start to whisper. Be quiet! Be quiet or Mum will take me to the doctor's or maybe she won't come back home.

Timmer curls up on his bean-bag. I pull my chair over to be near him. There's a drum in my head. It was all that drink last night. Ralph saved me. And Backwards-Dad saved Little Mikey. The room spins around me. Is Dad a good 'un or a bad 'un?

I groan because I can't work it out. The kitchen is too small. It's all wrong. No one is in the right place. I'm not staying here.

I draw a note for Pat to show I'm out with Timmer and walk into the garden. I clench my fists and then I start to run, run, run, run, run.

Where is Dad? What has he done? What has happened?

Timmer overtakes me as we go through the scrubland, over the ditch and into the field. Faster, Timmer, faster. There's a shadowy wind in my head and it's shrieking but I am going to outrun it and keep going. I put my arms out like

Little Mikey last night—I'm a plane and if I fall Dad will catch me. I keep running over the hill, past the river, along the woods, up the path and straight back to Cackler's farm.

I bend over double at the gates. My T-shirt is wet on my back. There are shiny snail trails across the gravel. My insides are firey and my legs ache but it feels good. I am smiling when I come up—right into Meg's face. She's standing next to me.

'Hello, stranger.' She's wearing a pink T-shirt today and her hair isn't tied back. It's really long and curly down her back and round her face.

'Meg!' I'm all fizzy and want to start running again but I stand still.

'You're up early.'

Timmer wags his tail and wriggles over to her.

'And look at the state of you!' Timmer's covered in sticky weed—he must have run through some on the way over. Meg starts to pull it off and he rolls over so she can rub his belly.

'My head hurt when I woke up so I went outside.'

Meg frowns. Timmer just lies still, waiting for her to start rubbing him again. 'You all right, Mikey?'

'I'm not supposed to drink.' I wipe my hands down my T-shirt because they are going all sweaty. 'I was out with the lads last night—and Ralph—and I had some beer.' I can feel my chest puff out when I say that.

Meg looks down. 'Oh, I see.'

She pulls a long bit of sticky weed off Timmer's leg. He's panting—must be hot. She stands for a minute, chewing her lip, then gets a bowl from the outhouse, fills it with water from the outside tap and puts it down for Timmer. He gulps and gulps and gulps.

'Are you good friends with Ralph then?'

'Yes!' I smile at her but Meg won't catch my eye. 'We found the tramp together, me and him . . . '

Meg wrinkles her nose. 'I'm sorry . . . must have been awful.'

I nod and swallow hard.

'But I wouldn't have met you if you hadn't come here and you wouldn't have seen Old Mary's calf being born if you hadn't . . . if . . . ' Meg grins suddenly. 'Come in and see how he's doing.'

'Who?'

'The calf.'

Meg throws some sticky weed at me. It gets stuck in my hair. She runs away, up to the field, as I pull it off. I shout and run after her.

I love Old Mary. You can see she's a good mum. Her calf is close by and Old Mary doesn't care if she winds up the other cows by hogging the best bit of the grass near the hedge—she's looking after him and that's that. Old Mary looks at me as we walk close. She remembers me, I know she does. Her brown eyes are so old they remember everything. She steps closer to the little calf though. *Don't mess with my baby*, she's saying.

I won't, Old Mary. I won't. I sit down a little way away from her and cross my legs. See? I am smaller than you now. I can't hurt you or your baby. Old Mary watches me for a minute and then starts to eat grass again. She lets the calf come round her so he's on the same side of her as me. That's her way of telling me she trusts me. I lie down and the sun shines hot on my face. I can even see the sunlight when I close my eyes.

Meg sits down next to me. I don't move. I keep still. That's what you do to make things trust you.

We don't say anything but it's a good quiet. The quiet like Timmer and me sitting in the shed. Or the quiet like Mum and me watching TV.

Suddenly Old Mary farts. Meg jumps, all surprised. She starts to giggle. Old Mary looks at me, really snooty, and turns away.

'Ooooh, poopy-doo!' Meg says, all silly.

I splurt out in giggles too. The calf skitters away from me. Old Mary looks at me, still snooty, and follows it. Then she does it again—a real ripper!

Meg rolls on her back, head back, snorting cos she's laughing so hard. My sides ache. Meg's curls are bobbing and she's all twinkly. I lean on my elbows and look at her. All the sunshine is singing.

'What are you two up to?' It's Cackler.

I sit up quick and so does Meg. I sneak a look at her out the corner of my eye—she's still laughing. I stand up. Cackler is tramping over the field towards us. He's wearing his funny floppy sunhat and carrying a walking stick even though he doesn't need one.

'Just checking up on Old Mary's calf, Gramps.' Meg runs over and hugs him. 'And Old Mary's full of methane . . .'

He pats her on the head and looks at me.

'She means, full of farts,' I say in case he's confused.

'Cows *are* windy creatures.' Cackler chuckles. 'Now, young Mikey, Old Mary is an excellent mother. It's not her that we need to keep an eye on. Bess is making a right mess of things as usual.'

As if she heard him, we hear her moo from lower down the field. Bess is pacing around, her eyes wide, calling for her calf. I look around the field. Where is your little one, Bess? Where is she? She calls again. Cows nearby start to shift around: they don't like to hear Bess so upset. I hate to hear it too. I screw up my face and look hard but I can't see her baby either.

Cackler is watching me really closely. 'Meg, your mum just phoned—wants you to call her back . . .'

Meg rolls her eyes, then runs back to the farm. Cackler puts his hand on my shoulder as we walk over to Bess.

'You helped Old Mary, remember, when she was calving?'

I nod. I remember. I saw her Backwards and helped her to feel calm.

'Think you could try to help out our Bess here too?'

'What? Help find her calf?'

Cackler nods. 'If you'd like to.'

I look at Bess's wide white eyes. 'I'll try.' I've never used the Backwards like this before—not to find answers. I nearly found out what happened to the tramp by the river but I didn't want to watch . . . But this is a good thing—this might help Bess and her baby, like the gentle Backwards helped Old Mary. My heart is starting to beat fast.

What do I do? What do I do? I clench my fists.

'Easy does it, Mikey. I think you know how to do this naturally.' Cackler's voice is quiet. 'You don't need to worry, lad.'

I stroke my arm so I feel better. This is important. I don't want to let Cackler or Bess down. The place has to tell me the secret—it has to show me the Backwards. I turn round slowly. Where shall I look? This field is huge.

I take a few steps uphill. The warm sun beats on my face. That doesn't feel right—it's normal there. I stand still. A cool wind ruffles my hair from behind me. I turn round.

Bess keeps pacing up and down at the bottom of the field by the hedge. I bet that's where she last saw her baby.

I walk closer. The field is waiting quietly for me. The sun is hot on my back but as I get closer to the hedge, cold stings my nose. The hairs on my arms stand up.

The world goes swirly. It's coming.

Bess's calf stands on the frosty grass right by the hedge.

I hold my hand up against the cold. Why is there frost again?

She's all alone. She goes a few steps one way, turns round and goes a few steps back. She cries out but can't see the other cows, just the other side of her field. There's a hole in the hedge. She stumbles, turns, walks through it on her skinny shaky legs.

I crouch down and push through to follow her, to see where she went. I'm a Backwards detective.

The calf looks round, doesn't know where to go. Bess's baby is in the wrong field. This is how she got lost.

I reach out but my hand passes straight through her. I can't touch things in the Backwards but I keep forgetting.

She cries again—her eyes wide.

I kneel down and wait. The sky gets darker. I hear Cackler in the Now on the other side of the hedge. He's watching me, his floppy hat poking above the hedge, but he doesn't follow. My hands are shaking.

The Backwards calf is off. She's heading the wrong way across this field towards the woods. Little frosty silver footprints.

I walk quietly next to her. I follow her as she stumbles towards the trees.

She's nearly there now. Slows down. I think she's getting tired. She has to pick her feet high to walk over the twigs and brambles. She cries for Bess again. It's no good, calf, turn round—you're going the wrong way! But she keeps going into the trees, looking for her mum.

There is a lot more frost in the woods.

I shiver. I want to go back now.

Branches cover the sky. I can't hear any birds. This isn't right. **Bess's calf is up ahead. She slips on some moss as she picks her way down a bank. She scrabbles with her legs but she isn't strong enough.**

I try to catch her, but I can't.

I see the frightened whites of her eyes as she tumbles. Legs, hooves, black-and-white-and-pink down to the bottom . . .

I run after her. My trainers are slippy on the ground, and I nearly fall over. I grab a branch but the brambles rip the skin on my arm as I skid past. Down, down, down . . . into a big dip in the ground . . . rolling over and over . . .

The rest of the wood is above me. It's a humungous hole. There are some big boulders down here just near the middle. There's ivy hanging down the slope on the other side. I still can't hear anything. No birds. No leaves rustling. Nothing.

I don't like it one bit.

I'm not staying here. I'm going back to get Cackler and Timmer. I look for Bess's calf quick before I start to climb back up the slope.

What's that? There's something on the ground just behind the smallest boulder. I go closer.

It's a hoof.

I move slowly step-by-step. *Here* she is! The calf has
hurt her leg. Her eyes are shut and she's curled up on the
ground against the rock. Her body moves up and down, up
and down. I hold my hand under her nose—the air goes
in and out. I touch her. She's warm. She's real. I've found
her! Here she is in the Now!

She doesn't move when I try to wake her up. Her
eyelids just flicker a bit. I try to lift her but she's too
heavy. I stand with my hands on the bottom of my back
and look up the steep bank. I need Cackler to help me
pick her up.

A cold wind blows in my face.

I move closer to the calf. Something is happening.
The world is starting to swirl again.

**I hear shouts in the wood above me. The sky is darker,
nearly night.**

I bend down. I want to hide.

**Someone crashes through the bushes above me, near
where the calf slipped on the moss. It's a man. All in black.**

The shadows behind me are starting to whisper. I
crouch down even more. I am still.

**He stops. He's listening. There are people behind him in
the wood shouting something but I can't hear them.**

I put my hand on the calf-belly and feel her breath go in and out, in and out.

The man starts sliding down the bank. Frost sparkles on the ground either side of him. He is coming this way. He is coming towards me.

This isn't good, this isn't good. I want Timmer. There's nowhere for me to run to.

The sun shines like moonlight. The man looks up to the stars and I see his face I see his face I see his face I see his face.

I dig the nails of my left hand into my right arm so that blood drips out.

Dad is here. He's come for me. He's going to get me because I ran away from him in the shed.

Shhhhh, shhhh, Mikey. Shhhhhhhhh.

I rock on my heels to feel better. Back and forth.

Dad's face is frightened. It's got black smudges on it. He smells of bonfires. The scar down his cheek is filled with shadows. The dark is eating him.

I snuggle closer to the calf. He hasn't seen me yet.

'Bill!' Dad whispers loudly, turning round and round.

I hide my face. I hear Dad walking towards me. I peep through my fingers.

'Bill, where are you?' His boots are scary-tough ones.

He's going to see me any moment. I wish the calf would wake up.

Dad is near my boulder. He spins round. I can see how

scared he is, even when he's looking the other way.

'Bill, we need to get going. Where are you?'

Dad is facing me. The boots get closer . . .

I close my eyes and hold my head and rock and rock and rock on my heels.

. . . And then he's behind me.

'Bill?' He's angry-frightened now.

Why didn't he talk to me? Didn't he see me?

Dad turns round and paces back towards me. He's looking panicky, all around the hole. His eyes go right over me.

There's a shout from the wood. Dad hears it. He runs straight through me and stands looking back up at the mossy bank.

A loud voice shouts down to us.

'Police! We have you surrounded!'

Dad spins round. His eyes look wild like the white-flashing-falling-calf-eyes.

'Bill,' he whispers and it sounds like he's going to cry, 'where are you, mate?'

Lots of men are standing around the top of the hole. Maybe six of them. The black-and-whites. Where have they all come from? The man shouts again—he's standing at the top of the mossy bank.

'It's no use making a run for it. Put your hands up.'

Dad jerks and runs a few steps forwards. There's a gun-clicking sound from the man above him.

'Stand still!'

Dad stops.

'Now, keep calm and no one gets hurt. Put your hands in the air.'

Dad sags. He lifts his arms but it looks like it's too much effort. One of the men skids down the bank to him, pulls his hands behind his back and I hear another click. Handcuffs.

'C'mon, son. Back the way you came.' This man's voice is deep and a bit friendly.

I see Dad's face before they march him up the bank and away through the woods. His eyes are squinted half-shut and he is shaking his head like he just can't believe it. He looks broken.

I move forwards at a distance. No one takes any notice of me.

Dad is yanked up the bank. Scuffles. Snapping twigs. Men disappear back into the dark of the wood.

I shiver; someone else is here.

I look up.

There's someone—another man—hiding behind a tree up there. I can't see him properly in the dark. He's been watching everything too. He waits till the noise of the police and Dad has gone, then he steps back quietly and is gone.

My head spins.

I sit down.

A warm breeze ruffles my hair. It ruffles the leaves

in the trees too—they are sighing back to life—and the branches sway above me against the blue blue sky. A blackbird twitters and lands on one of the boulders. It's standing in a bit of sunlight.

It's time for me to go to fetch help for Bess's calf.

The Backwards is gone.

Chapter Twelve

'I've found her! She's in the woods!' I wave at Cackler. He's in the cow field, mending the hole in the hedge with wire. He puts his tools down and walks over to me. The sun is high in the sky and it's making my arms red. I'm getting thirsty too.

'I knew you could do it,' he says quietly, when he reaches me. He takes the floppy hat off and wipes his sleeve over the top of his bald head. 'Now, show me where this little rascal got to and I'll bring her home.'

Cackler follows me into the woods back to the dip in the ground.

I point over to the boulder. 'She's there. See her?'

'Ah, yes! Would you believe it!' Cackler picks up the calf and rests her across his shoulders. He's strong—he climbs up that bank with her like he's just climbing the

118

stairs to bed. No bother at all. It's safe now he's here in the woods. Everything is safe around Cackler. The calf knows it too and she's woken up.

'I'll just get the vet to check her out but I think she'll be all right.' He catches my eye and smiles. 'Thanks to you, Mikey.'

I go all tingly.

'Well, thanks to you and your special gift, that is.'

I stand still. 'What do you mean?'

Cackler is careful as he lifts his foot above some brambles. He goes steady so that he doesn't have to hold on to anything to keep straight. Then he lifts the other leg. He's over with no problem and waits for me. I get caught by bramble-arms and pull my leg hard. My jeans rip.

'Easy does it, lad. Easy does it.' Cackler looks at me and smiles. 'I mean that you know things about animals so that you can help them, don't you?' His brown face crinkles up. 'That's a gift, Mikey. A gift.'

'You think so?'

'Don't you?'

I don't know. The Backwards isn't always happy.

'Hey.' Cackler puts his hand on my arm. He stops walking. 'You helped Bess's calf. You helped Old Mary. That's a good thing, Mikey. A good thing.'

'But sometimes, I see other things too. Bad things.'

I saw Backwards-Dad here. Someone brought the black-and-whites to get him. His mate was supposed to meet him here and he never did. I can't say anything to Cackler because of the Golden Rule and I can't talk about the Backwards because people won't like me and I don't know what to say to Cackler now but it WAS all right with the little cows, wasn't it? It was, wasn't it?

'It was a good thing that happened today.' Cackler watches me until I stop rocking from side to side and look back at him. His eyes are old old old and they know things. 'Even if what you can do is different, it doesn't matter.' His eyes smile. 'It doesn't matter, Mikey. It's all right.'

My lip is going all wobbly but I smile back. Cackler nods at the calf on his shoulders.

'Bess'll be saying thank you to you too. She's a funny mother, that one, letting her little one wander all over the place, not knowing where her baby is.'

We step out into the field. It's sunny again. I like it now I'm away from all that frost and the woods and the Dad stuff.

'It's best with animals.'

'What did you say, young Mikey?' Cackler raises his eyebrows.

'My gift thing. It's best with animals, not people.'

'Maybe,' Cackler shrugs. 'I'm an animal-man myself, like you, but don't limit yourself, Mikey. Let things run their course.'

Bess is waiting on the other side of the hedge. She makes humphing noises as we get closer. The calf starts jiffling on Cackler's shoulders. I do some twirls. I want to laugh. No one has believed the Backwards before.

Cackler puts the calf on the ground. She only has to walk a little way to the field so she should be able to manage on her own. Her legs are shaky but she's OK. Bess leans over to her to get closer to her, to stop her being upset.

'But what if I find other things—things that I don't like?'

Bess starts to lick her calf.

'You were looking for Bess's calf and you found her.' Cackler pulls his hat straight to shade his eyes from the sun. 'Do you think you were maybe looking for those other things if you found them too?'

My heart thumps. I've never seen Dad's Backwards like that before. *Was* I looking for Dad? My head hurts. I don't know. I'm scared of him but I miss him too. I don't like this question.

Cackler strokes his chin, watching me carefully. 'Sometimes things seem bad but really they're helping you get better.' He pulls his pipe out of his pocket and knocks it against a tree to empty it. He looks up and smiles at me. 'Nature always heals, Mikey. Always. Just let it come.'

I feel what Cackler says right in my belly. I let out a deep breath.

Cackler nods as if he's heard me thinking. He pats his jacket pockets until he finds his tobacco pouch—pulls it out. 'It always makes me feel better when I remember that.'

A dog howls from a few fields away. Timmer. I'd recognize his voice anywhere. He's been on his own, tied up all morning. He'll hate it.

'I've got to go, Cackler! I've got to go home now the calf is OK again!'

Cackler shakes his head, pipe in mouth, and waves at me as I run down the field.

'Well, suit yourself then, see if I care!'

I can hear the smiles in his voice as it follows me down the hill.

Chapter Thirteen

Timmer's going mad now he's free again. I love watching him go full-throttle across the field, ears forward, like he can run for ever.

I put a piece of grass between my thumbs and blow to make a loud noise. Timmer barks and charges towards me. I do it again. He barks, stands still, then runs into the trees. I see a flash of white. Bunny tail. He's chasing a rabbit but he'll never catch it. It had a good head start.

It makes me feel funny, looking into the trees. Dad was set up in these woods so the black-and-whites got him. I never knew that. Someone was a bad 'un to Dad. I shiver. I like what Cackler said about the Backwards though. My gift?

I turn round when I get to the scrubland-before-the-fields and look over at his farm. I can hardly see it now, except for a little bit of red roof behind the trees. The cows are white dots on the green field above the farmhouse. Two of those dots will be Bess and her baby, together again. My stomach goes warm when I think that. I helped. The Backwards helped. I did good today.

I wish me and Mum were together again like that. I wish I could make her better and want to come home.

Timmer is scratching at a hole near the railings. I bend down to look at it. Rabbit hole. There are loads of them round here. He barks, looks up, black ear flopping over, then starts digging with his front legs. Dirt flying everywhere. Timmer looks up again. You've got muck all over your nose, you scruffy hound! He wags his tail and keeps digging.

I'm not waiting here to get covered in dirt, Timmer-dog!

I pick up an empty plastic bottle and bash it down the railings along the bottom of some gardens. It makes a cool drummy sound. I do it again. If you look down the railings, it looks like bars. Prison. Clanging. I drop the bottle quick. I turn slowly and look across the scrubland and the fields. Are you out there, Dad? Are you?

I go back into my garden and sit down. I smooth down the grass—Mum smooths things, tablecloths and stuff, when she's thinking too, usually after she's been looking at the photos. I press my hands down to the earth underneath. It's cool. Some ants crawl over my thumb.

Mum looks at the photos because she misses Dad. He's done something wrong—I heard her on the phone. The shadows in the bushes start to whisper. *Mum* says he's still in prison but I saw him in the shed. Cackler believes me that the Backwards is real.

What if . . . I take a deep breath . . . what if I try to find out for sure? Use the Backwards, use my gift, to find out if he's still in prison. Timmer walks up the garden, wagging his tail. His face is covered in dirt. You'll help me, won't you? You will make sure I'm OK?

I'm NOT doing the prison Backwards—that's when all the Backwards stuff started and it's a black black Backwards in prison. I scrunch my toes in my shoes and make my fingers go stiff. I'm NEVER doing that again. Never.

I stay very still. How could I find out then?

There was a nice lady prison-black-and-white who looked after me when I tried to visit Dad once. She wrote her name in the Prison Visity Book they gave me. I haven't got that book any more but I know how to see it in the Backwards.

My chest goes tight. It won't be nice Backwards though.

I put my hands round my head really gently. 'S OK, Mikey. 'S OK. Cackler said sometimes bad things make you feel better. Then you can find Dad, just like you found the calf. Then Mum will come home. Then we can all go to the beach and be happy like in the photo. Come on, Mikey. Come on. Just get it over with. Then it's done. Timmer will be there too so you'll be safe and if it's really bad, you can just run away from it. Just run away.

I try the back door. It's locked. Pat's gone out. Good. I unlock it and go straight upstairs, step by step up the brown flowery carpet. My heart is beating like a mad mad drum. I'm doing this for Mum and for Dad and for me and for Little Mikey. I stop at the top step and take a deep breath.

I stand outside Little Mikey's bedroom. Timmer sits down quietly next to me. I haven't been in here for a long time. I hold Timmer's collar and push my fingers into his fur.

'I'm trying to find out where Dad is,' I whisper to Timmer. 'I'm trying to use the Backwards like I did for Bess.'

He wags his tail and looks up at me.

'But if it's too bad, we'll just get out quick, OK?'

The shadows behind the door are moving, getting louder. They make my belly clench. They make my head feel black.

'I'm not going to run away from them, this time, Timmer. Stay close, doggy. Stay close.'

Timmer thumps his tail on the floor.

'Ready?'

I push the door open a little bit. It's cold like opening the freezer.

Everything is covered with thick frost . . . Look, Timmer!

Chapter Thirteen

The Man. United flag at the window, teddy on the floor, the half-built model plane on the table . . . And over there, over there . . . there he is . . .

I yank the door shut. I don't like this. My heart is drumming so loud my ears nearly burst. Timmer presses into me, warm and safe. He looks up at me with his brown quiet eyes. I let the world settle again. A car passes in the street. Someone slams a door shut. Everyday noises, here and now.

I take a deep breath. The Now will be waiting for me—I can come back to it any time I like. I can shut the door again if I want to, can't I? I hold Timmer's collar tight, push down the handle and step onto the blue bedroom carpet.

Little Mikey is sitting on the floor in the corner squashed between his bed and the wall. He's got snot hanging out of his nose, his eyes are red, he's really white and he's rocking rocking rocking back and forth, back and forth.

My eyes sting. He's changed. He's not normal Little Mikey because he's got the scar now.

Mum is sitting on his Spiderman duvet next to him, stroking his hair. She's smiling that smile with tears in it. I hate it when she does that—it means she wants Dad but pretends she doesn't.

'Don't worry, love. Shhhhhhhh, there there . . . '

He's so frightened. Look after him, Mum. Look after him.

'Oh love, my Mikey,' she's almost singing. She sits down

next to him on the floor by the bed. She can hardly fit in with him but I know Little Mikey likes how squished he is, close and warm up to her. She's so cuddled up he can't rock any more. Mum puts her arm round him and strokes his curly hair. Little Mikey's twitching gets slower.

'I can't.' His voice is bubbly with the tears and the snot.

'I know, love. It was a bad idea.' Mum pulls a tissue from up her sleeve and wipes his nose. Little Mikey doesn't notice. 'I shouldn't have let you go. It wasn't the right time.'

'I can't.' His face scrunches up. 'I can't . . . ' he's whispering now.

'I know, I'm sorry, love. I'm sorry.' Mum's lips are all smudgy as she kisses the top of his head.

Tears are dripping down Little Mikey's face again. His fists are tight—he's getting ready to fight someone no one else can see.

'You don't have to go back there, Mikey, to that prison. Not unless you want to.'

Little Mikey cries out like a little animal. Mum hugs him close. She thinks he's just crying but he isn't. His mouth is moving but she can't see it. He's saying things without talking but she can't hear him.

But I want to see my dad, he says.

'It's a terrible thing he did. I could kill him, sometimes, I could kill him for what he's done to us.'

But I want to see my dad. I just wanted to see him.

'That bloody place is enough to make anyone upset.'

He belongs here with us.

'You and me, we don't need him. We just don't need this, this . . . ' Mum shakes her fist to the ceiling.

Little Mikey cries out again. 'Mum, I hate that book. I hate it!'

Mum rubs his back, then strokes his face, then kisses his nose—she can't decide which bit she needs to hug to make him better. 'Which book, love? Which one?'

'The Prison Visity Book. I hate it. I HATE IT!'

Little Mikey flings his head back hard to hit it against the wall but Mum catches him just in time.

'It's OK, love. It's OK. I'll get rid of the book, don't worry.'

'NOW! Do it NOW! Burn it! BURN IT!' Little Mikey screams and flings his head back again.

Mum catches him in time but only just. She holds his face and pulls her face close to his. She's not cross but she's serious. She speaks in a quiet voice so Little Mikey has to stop shouting to hear her.

'I will get rid of it, love. I will burn it if you like. But you take a deep breath now. It's time to calm down. No more of this, love. No more. I'm not having you hurt yourself. No, I'm not.'

Little Mikey sags a bit.

'That's it, love, that's it. Deep breaths, deeeep breaths.'

His chest goes up . . . and down . . . up . . . and down. His eyes are quiet. He pulls the book out from under the bed.

It's the story of children going to visit people in prison—all in pictures you have to colour in. The black-and-whites. The rooms you wait in. The rooms you see Dad in. The bars. The keys. It's supposed to get you ready but it doesn't. The book lied. Little Mikey knows it. I know it. Mum knows it too. The book doesn't tell you about the black black Backwards in there that makes you shake. It doesn't tell you about the shadows. Or the smells. Or the clanging. It lied. It lied. Burn it, Mum. Get rid of it.

Mum pulls the metal bin in front of her. She pulls out her cigarette lighter. Just for a minute she stops. Flicks the pages. Get on with it! Get on with it! BURN IT! Burn the black black Backwards so it's gone for ever.

I lie on the bed, lean over Mum's shoulder. I can see my scribbly baby-writing, my wonky colouring-in.

She turns to the page with the waiting-room on it. There's the picture of the lady black-and-white with her name written underneath it. Her name is, her name is . . . stay still, Mum, stop turning the pages . . . **it's Prison Officer Jane Smith.**

Prison Officer Jane Smith.

Jane. I like that name. It's smiley. She was smiley. She held my hand and smelt of roses secretly underneath all the black clothes and she helped me to get out quick when the Backwards came.

The lighter flicks into life. I lean forwards with Little

130

Mikey. Mum holds the book over the paper bin. She holds the flame at the corner of the book. For a minute nothing happens. Then the flames curl up. They start to eat the paper. Up and up they go, leaving black stuff where the paper is burned off. That book was bad. The prison was bad.

She drops it into the paper basket. It burns quickly. It's nearly gone. Mum picks up Little Mikey's glass of night-time-drinking-water. She pours it into the bin. It sizzles like sausages under the grill.

The book has gone.

'OK, Mikey?'

Little Mikey has a tired white smile.

'Come downstairs with me, then, and we'll watch some telly. Let's forget all this now.'

She humphs as she stands up and straightens her skirt.

Little Mikey is slower. He drags his feet as he follows her to the bedroom door. I can hear Mum walking downstairs, her slippers are slapping against her bare feet. Little Mikey looks for a minute longer at the waste-paper basket. Then he looks straight at me. It's like he can see me.

'Mikey! Come on, love! Want to watch TV with some pop and crisps as a treat?'

He moves out of the room slowly and his mouth is wobbly. His lips move—he's speaking without talking again.

But I still want my dad, he whispers.

Then he leaves the room and lets the door close softly behind him.

Pat calls up the stairs. 'Been to see your mum at Gran's, Mikey! She sends her love! No need to phone her tonight! Doctor says she just needs some rest—will be fine again soon.'

I leave Little Mikey's room with Timmer and make sure the door clicks shut. I stick my head over the banister. She's sweating so her rainbow face is twinkling.

'When is she coming back?'

'Not long now. Fish'n'chips for tea and then I've got a DVD from the shop for us to watch. What do you say?'

I look down at Timmer. That means we'll have to wait until tomorrow to call Prison Officer Jane Smith, Timmer-dog. We'll wait until Pat goes to check on her own house in the morning and then we'll do it. May be that's good because I'm still shaky from that Backwards.

I look at the closed door to Little Mikey's bedroom before I go downstairs. We were brave to go in there, Tim-mer-dog. Brave. And even though I'm wobbly, the shadows have gone quieter in there now. I hold my hand over my heart and feel the beat, beat, beat. It's strange but I can feel that something else in me has gone very soft and sad and still.

Prison Officer Jane Smith. Prison Officer Jane Smith.

The door slams and Pat walks down the path. I hold the phone in both hands. I'm sitting in the corner on the floor down the side of my bed. I must phone now while the house is still empty. Timmer turns in circles and makes a little dog-nest in my duvet—it's fallen onto the carpet next to my feet.

I dial the number from Mum's phone book very carefully. I check each number two times before I press the button. This is important. My hands are shaking. I have to get it right. The phone is ringing. My stomach is panicking. My head is panicking. I listen very hard for a voice.

'Redbridge Prison, how can I help?' It's a woman. That's good. 'Hello? Can I help you?'

What do I say? What do I say?

'I'm phoning to see if I can talk to my dad.'

'Is your dad in the prison?'

'Yes.'

'What's his name?'

The questions jab but I take a deep breath. 'Stu Baxter. That's his name.'

'An inmate?'

'Yes.'

'Hmmmmmmmm. Do you have another parent or a social worker? Someone to make this arrangement?'

'No.'

'How old are you, please?'

The questions are too quick. What does this mean? Why does it matter? 'Fourteen.'

'You need to go through a special procedure to make this arrangement you know.'

'Is Prison Officer Jane Smith there please?'

'Sorry?'

'She helped me last time.'

'I'll have to check but you need a grown-up, your mum or someone like that, to sort this out for you.'

There's a big gulp in my throat that I can't swallow. I was brave and went into the scary Backwards to find out her name. I want to talk to Dad. Mum isn't here. I have to do this on my own. There isn't anyone to help me.

'Prison Officer Jane Smith said she'd help me talk to Dad.' My voice is really low.

'Can I take your name?'

'I just want to talk to Dad.'

'I know. I know it's hard but can I take your name, please?'

'Is Dad there?'

The lady goes quiet on the phone, then rustles some papers. Maybe she's checking lists.

'You need to talk to your mum. Is she with you?'

'No. She's out. Can I talk to Prison Officer Jane Smith, please?' My voice is starting to wobble but I try to keep it straight so that the lady can hear what I'm saying. 'She said she'd help me see him whenever I was ready.'

'I don't think she still works here. I'll check. Just one moment please . . . '

I swallow hard. I tried but I'm just too stupid. Too STUPID to work anything out. I hit the floor with my fist. I can hear a cry come out of my mouth before I can stop it.

'You all right there?'

'I want to talk to my dad.'

'I'm sorry, this information is protected . . . '

Another sob pushes up from my chest.

'Is there someone there who can . . . oh God . . . you poor little mite . . . '

'My dad . . . ' I whisper.

'I'm just going to put you on hold—I'll be back in a moment. OK?'

'OK . . . '

There are some beeps down the phone, but it doesn't go completely quiet. I can still hear the lady talking but she's far away and she's speaking to someone else. 'Is the Family Liaison Officer back now? This boy wants to see his dad Stu Baxter but—look at this list—he's not actually *in* the prison at the moment . . . '

I freeze when I realize what she's said. I can't speak. There's some rustling, the voices are going further and further away. I let the phone drop.

'Hello?' The lady is back and her voice is loud again. 'Are you still there? Hello? Hello?'

I watch the phone. I reach out with my bare foot. My big toe presses the red button on the phone and the lady is gone.

I look over at Timmer. Dad's not there. He's not in prison. It's true. I was right.

Dad has escaped.

Chapter Fourteen

I walk as hard as I can across the fields at the back of the house. My legs are extra-strong because I am angry angry ANGRY. The sky is blue but I can see the Backwards thunderclouds forming and I don't care. *Now* what do I do? I don't know! I DON'T KNOW!

I'm fed up with the Backwards. I'm fed up with Dad and prison and burning and Mum and crying and shadows and scars. The shadows start to shriek anyway. I ignore them. Timmer yaps. There's a wind blowing but I can't work out if it's Now or then but I don't care anyway because I can't sort it out. Stupid Mikey. I stamp my foot hard on the grass. Timmer barks. The wind whips around me and it's cold. Bitey-teeth cold.

Fine.

Fine.

Get on with it then. Bring it on then. See if I care. See if I care about ANYTHING.

I run to the riverbank. **The Backwards sky is night-dark. The tramp is standing next to me. He's shorter than me. And fat. His hat is wonky and he's reaching out towards me with his old wrinkly dirty hands. His beard has drips in it. He looks sorry about something.**

Well, you can just get lost! Just get lost will you?

I walk hard towards the bridge, towards the bit of the river where we found his body. **He is running along beside me—all jolty and funny.**

'Don't follow me! Leave me alone!' I shout at him.

The shadows are dancing like nutters in my head. My eyes ache. My scar aches. Argggggggh!! I hold my head and I howl to the skies like a wolf.

Timmer cries with me and the Backwards clouds swirl.

But the tramp keeps on going. He's running. He's ignoring me. He's in the Backwards and he doesn't even know that I'm watching him.

The scream sticks in my throat.

He's in his Backwards.

The tramp is scared. He's running along the riverbank. This is where he dies. This is where it happens. He's running away from someone and that person is behind me.

I pull my hair so hard that my eyes start to cry. The riverbank is trying to tell me its big secret. It's so big that it's spilling out all around for me to see.

The murderer is behind me.

Turn round, Mikey. Turn round and see who it is. But I can't. I'm scared. I breathe in hard and the cold is sharp like broken glass. I can't do this. I reach down for Timmer and squeeze the scruff of his neck hard.

The moon is high in the sky. The tramp is puffing, he's struggling. No one is here to help him.

Turn round, Mikey. Turn round.

Someone runs past me, following the tramp. He gives a kind of grunt as he runs. My whole body is as stiff as a post. My eyes blur. I don't want to watch. **He's fast. He's catching the tramp up easily.** I can't, can't, CAN'T watch this. The world is falling. I'm falling. I'm on my knees and the grass is wet. My head leans on it. Grass tickles my face. I cover my ears. I listen to the pumping sound in them. I listen to my breath. In and out. I feel Timmer next to me. I make a moany noise.

What is happening to the tramp near the bridge? I can't save him. I can't watch. I can't do anything. The Backwards is too big for me.

'Mikey? Is that you?'

I recognize that voice. Timmer growls. I open my eyes. It's night-time and it's sunny. There are dark clouds and blue skies. There's something terrible happening near the bridge but it's not there any more.

I groan again and roll over in a ball.

'You all right, mate?'

A shadow falls on me. I look up. It's Ralph. My mate Ralph. I smile but I sort of want to cry too.

The Backwards dark is going. It's hot on the back of my T-shirt. I sit up. Just for a minute, I feel swirly in my head but then the swirls go. It's bright. It's the Now again. I look up the riverbank to the bridge. Empty.

'What you doing down there, Mikey? Come on, mate. Come back to the farm with me.' He holds out his hand to pull me up.

I don't move for a minute. Timmer stands between me and Ralph. His ears are flat and pressed back. Who was the man chasing the tramp? Who was it? Was it Dad? I only saw the back of him running so I don't know. I couldn't look properly. The tramp—he *knew* who it was. I look back towards the bridge.

Just for a minute, I see the tramp's frightened face, looking up and lifting his hands to cover his head as he crouches low.

At the back of my mind, somewhere in the fog, I can feel the shape of an idea. I screw my face up.

'Mikey?'

The shape goes woolly and floats away at the edges. I don't know what it was. It's gone now anyway.

Ralph keeps watching me out of the corner of his eye as we walk along the riverbank towards the farm. I haven't seen the bittern for a few days. Timmer keeps so close to me he's nearly tripping me up. There's so much space here, why don't you use it instead of getting under my feet, stupid mutt?

'What was wrong back there, Mikey?' Ralph doesn't look at me when he asks the question, but I can tell all his body is waiting for my answer.

'I'm having a bad day.' I clench my fists.

'Want to tell your old mate Ralph about it?' He still looks straight ahead, his footsteps keep in time with mine.

'I think it's a secret.'

'Up to you, mate. You just seem upset.' Ralph looks over at me and smiles. 'But if it helps, I keep lots of secrets, I do.'

I believe him. I think he likes secrets—you can tell by his sparky eyes. But he's all right, is Ralph. He saved me from the lads at the pub garden.

'See . . . ' I clasp my fingers round my head, 'I reckon . . . I reckon . . . ' I can't quite finish what I want to say. My head is foggy because Mum always says not to talk to anyone about Dad, doesn't she? Our Golden Rule.

'What, mate?'

I shake my head but the shadows in there make me sick.

Ralph nods slowly. We're at the track running down to Cackler's farm now.

'Look, Mikey, it's nearly my lunch-break. Might knock

off early—my house is just over there. I can see you're upset. Why don't you come over with me? Have a sarnie? That little job I told you about has come up now and I can tell you about it too, if you like.'

Sunshine blasts my head. Did you hear that, Timmer? Oi, Timmer! I *never* go round to people's houses and he just asked me! Just like that! I do my little knee-bendy dance and squeeze my hands together.

'That'd be brilliant, BRILLIANT, Ralph!'

He laughs. 'Come on then, mate. This way . . . ' He waves his hand down the track through the edge of the woods and starts off in front of me.

I turn round to look for Timmer. He's facing the other way, down the riverbank towards the bridge, and his whole body is tight—he's watching something. I hear the far away crackle of footsteps in frost and shiver.

There's the tramp, with his black coat and his black hat, standing facing me, facing Ralph.

NO! Not now. I'm with my mate, Ralph. I'm going round to his house. I'M NOT HAVING THIS AGAIN TODAY.

'C'mon, boy. Leave it, Timmer, this way.'

Timmer gives a low whine and turns round, head on one side.

'TIMMER!'

He paws the ground and whines again. Fine! Follow when you're ready. Ralph starts to whistle and I just see the red of his T-shirt as he turns round the corner out of view. I run to catch up. I look back quickly. Timmer is following me.

But the tramp figure is still standing there, watching, waiting.

Chapter Fifteen

There are three old council houses up here. I'd forgotten about them. I thought they were all empty anyway because Albert said they were going to be pulled down for some posh new place or something.

Ralph goes up the little path of the middle one. It has a blue front door but the paint is coming off, like on my shed. The front garden is all weeds and there's an old black mini with plants growing inside it parked under an old tree that looks like it's died. The garden is even messier than ours.

He beckons me in. 'Home sweet home, mate.'

'That your car?'

'Oh, that old thing?' Ralph looks over at it and wipes his sleeve across his forehead. 'Yeah, it looks a bit of a mess but I was going to fix it up, like, and make it work again. They're back in fashion, minis.' He runs his hands through his hair and shakes his head. 'It's just finding the time, though, mate. Never enough time.' He turns to walk back into the house.

'You could fix it? Dad . . . ' I want to say that Dad was brilliant and he fixed cars all the time. He could do car-magic, he said, and bring any car back to life. I do a jump inside: I never normally remember things Dad said.

Ralph stops and looks at me in a funny way. He frowns. 'Course I could fix it, Mikey. I was a mechanic before I worked for Cackler. Didn't you know that?'

I shake my head. He starts to say something, then stops, then starts again.

'C'mon in, mate, c'mon in.'

There aren't any carpets inside and it smells funny—a bit like a bathroom when you forgot to open the window after a shower. There are dirty black marks in the corners, sort of massive blobby spider's webs sucked into the walls. I stop in the hallway. Something isn't right in here. My head is starting to ache again. Timmer stands at the doorway, still growling.

'Through here, Mikey!' Ralph is in the kitchen at the end and there's more sunshine up there. He's at this old rickety table with sticky pots all over it, making jam sandwiches. There's no proper stuff in here—like kitchen cupboards—it's all little tables and odd chairs and piles of things. There is a funny little fridge and an old cooker though.

I step into the room and shiver. The shadows are loud in here. They are hissing around me.

'Cold?' Ralph notices me shivering. 'We can eat outside. Warmer out there.' He passes me a plate with the sandwiches and a packet of ready-salted crisps. I don't really like ready-salted but I don't say anything. Ralph has made me lunch and that was kind and he's my mate.

Timmer is still waiting at the front door. We sit on some old green plastic barrels by the front window. The sun is hot. Ralph rolls up the sleeve of his shirt. His arms are really brown and muscly. I can see the naked curvy woman again. He laughs when he sees me looking at it.

'Like my girlfriend, do you?' He takes a swig of Coke.

My face burns. I look down and pick the crusts off the edge of the sandwich. A wasp lands on my hand trying to get at the jam. I put a bit on the crust and leave it on the ground. The wasp goes for it. Ralph laughs.

'You got a girlfriend, Mikey? Good-looking lad like you must be fighting them off with a stick.'

I shake my head but I still don't look up at him.

'I reckon Meg quite likes you, you know.'

I can feel him watching me. I want him to stop talking now. Everything is red and hot. I think of Meg touching my arm and the calf being born and the blood and her smiling at me as I left the farm. It makes me dizzy.

I look up slowly and wrinkle my nose because I can't think what to say.

146

Chapter Fifteen

Ralph throws his head back and laughs in a loud voice and slaps me on the back.

'Ah, you're a rum 'un, Mikey boy.'

I laugh too but I want to hide the things I think about Meg—sort of put my arms round them, like some people do around their books when they're writing at school so no one can see what they are doing. I put one of the crisps in my mouth but it isn't crunchy—it's soft. I don't like them.

Something dark out the corner of my eye makes me jump. A black cat whizzes out of the old mini and rushes up the garden path. Timmer yelps and runs after it. The cat is already climbing up the apple tree. Ralph laughs.

'When are you going to mend the car, then?' I ask. Dad said that a car that doesn't work is sad—it's sort of dead or ill or something. I frown; I've thought about Dad-things twice now in Ralph's garden. I wait for the shadows to start to chatter but they don't. I feel an ache inside but it's not in my head.

'Dunno, mate. Look,' he turns to face me and puts down his plate, 'there's something I want to show you. I didn't realize that you didn't know . . .'

'Know what?'

'Hang on. Back in a sec.' Ralph wipes his hands down his jeans and goes into the house.

Timmer walks back slowly and slumps at my feet.

I stroke his ears, smooth and soft. I don't know why you don't like Ralph, Timmer. He's just given me lunch and now he's showing me things. We're mates.

Ralph is back and he's carrying some paper. 'About when I was a mechanic.' He sits on his barrel and hands it to me. 'Just think that you ought to know something.'

I look at it. It's a photo taken in front of the old garage before it was burned down. I feel cold. I never go there any more. It's full of sad Backwards. Timmer pushes close. There are three men in the photo, standing next to a red Volkswagen Golf. There's Dad in his work overalls, smiling and brown from being outside so much, and there—with his arm round Dad's neck—is Ralph. My mate Ralph is in the photo wearing overalls too.

I put the photo down. I want to cry. I stand up. I make my fingers go stiff. Dad smiles up at me from the photo. Dad and Ralph.

'Hey, Mikey, it's OK, mate. It's OK.' Ralph reaches out to me but I don't want him to touch me because I need to think and because I don't understand what this is all about. Why didn't I know Ralph worked with Dad? Why has he shown me this? What does it mean? I hear myself let out a moan.

Ralph holds up his hands and steps away from me.

''S OK, mate, 's OK. I just thought you might like to know that we're all mates. I'm mates with you. I was mates with your dad. That's good isn't it? Hey, Mikey?'

Chapter Fifteen

Is that good? Is that good? The lads were mean to me in the pub and they wanted to be mates and it wasn't good. I look at the photo. Dad was smiling and I want to cry but he *was* smiling so that means he was happy to be with Ralph. Ralph and me and Dad. All mates together. Is that right?

'You get it, Mikey? We were all mates. Nothing to be worried about. Nothing has changed. OK?'

He smiles at me. Ralph is looking out for me. He's helping me again. He's always helping me. I've never had such a good friend. I smile.

'OK. OK, Ralph.' I reach over and nearly hug him but then I pat his arm, just near the naked curvy lady but not on her, and sit down.

''S just you seemed so upset today and I wanted to cheer you up. Y'know, when I found you by the riverbank.' Ralph sits down too but he's looking at me out the corner of his eye. The wind is waking up. It blows in the trees in the next-door garden and two blackbirds fly up into the sky. 'I was your dad's pal. If I can help and you want to talk to me, you can, you know.'

This morning—that was when I found out Dad had escaped and then I saw the tramp running along the riverbank just before, just before . . . My eyes prickle. Timmer leans against me. All these things I don't understand, all blurry and tangly. Ralph smiles. He'll help me. He knew Dad anyway—he started talking about him so I'm not breaking the Golden Rule, am I?

'It's about Dad,' I whisper. Timmer growls, ears back. Quiet, boy, I need some help with this and Ralph is our mate.

Ralph doesn't say anything but he nods. He's watching me carefully with his brown eyes. His eyes are so strong I wonder if they can see the Backwards in my head, all swirling about. He takes another swig of his Coke. I lean forward and whisper.

'I think he's escaped from prison.'

Ralph's eyebrows shoot up and he coughs on his Coke so it splutters all over the garden. He pats his chest. His eyes water.

'Sorry, Mikey—you caught me by sur—' he coughs again. 'Why do you say that, mate?'

'I phoned the prison and they said he's not there any more.'

'Ah.' He closes his eyes and rubs either side of the top of his nose with his thumb and forefinger. 'I see. You're looking for him?'

My voice is so small I hardly hear myself say 'Yes.'

Eyes still closed, Ralph says, 'Look, we're mates, aren't we?'

I nod.

'Tell you what, I'll help you find your dad—pull some strings as it were, if you like, what do you say?'

'You would? You WOULD? Ralph? Ralph?'

Ralph opens his eyes. 'Yes, mate. I would. You mind doing me a little favour in return?'

'Anything, Ralph! Anything!' I'm squeezing my knees with my hands so tight that it hurts.

'You're a good man, Mikey, a good man.' Ralph smiles. 'It's only a little thing though.' He leans forwards, arms on his legs, like he's telling something important to another man. I do the same thing. 'Those boys you were with in the Horse and Hounds . . .'

'Dave and Jim and Toby?'

'Yeah, that's right. They're your friends, right?'

I nod slowly. I *think* they are . . . they wanted me to join their gang . . . but then it went wrong.

'Well, that Dave—he's made life difficult for me recently—you know?'

I don't know. I don't know at all.

'You had to down-in-one too?'

'No, mate, no drinks. Just . . . trouble. So I need you to find out when Dave next plans on going to that pub and let me know—OK?'

'That's easy! Sure, Ralph!'

'Good lad! You come to the farm—or here—and let me know when you've found out, right?'

'And you'll tell me where Dad is?'

Ralph nods.

I hold out my hand. We need to shake on this. This is important. Ralph takes my hand but his shoulders are shaking and he's smiling.

'C'mon, then. Time for me to get back to work.'

As he stands up, I look back down at the photo. Dad and Ralph. Dad and Ralph. And the other man. There's another man in the photo too. He's short and has a big nose and pale blue eyes. I don't know him but I do know him. Who is he, Timmer? Who is that man?

'Bloody hell, is that the time?' Ralph looks at his watch. 'Got to rush, mate, got to rush. Delivery of cattle feed due any minute and Cackler's out today. See you later, yeah?'

He starts to run down the path, whistling that tune again. Timmer and me follow him down the garden path but I go slowly. It's bothering me. I *know* that other man.

I stand for a moment at the gatepost, looking back at the house and the black mini. The wind is still up in the trees. Timmer barks. I shiver. I'm coming, Timmer-dog. We've got a job to do now. We've got to find Dave. Timmer wags his tail and runs up the path, back through the woods.

I try to copy Ralph's whistle as I follow but it doesn't sound quite right.

Chapter Sixteen

Pat's sitting in the lounge when I get home, chatting on the phone. She's already wearing her dressing-gown even though it's only tea-time. She smiles when she sees me. Her face looks ill because there are no colours painted on it.

'Hey! There's someone here to talk to you!' Pat passes me the phone.

'Hello?'

'Mikey! It's me, Mum. How are you, love?'

'Mum! It's you!! I miss you!' I don't like hearing her far away. 'When are you coming home?'

'Soon. Miss you too, Mikey. I've not been well. Are things OK with Pat?'

I can hear her too-bright smile down the phone.

'S'pose.' It's not the same but I can't say that because Pat's listening. 'What's wrong?'

Nothing. Then a gurgly noise.

'Are you crying? . . . Mum? . . . Mum?'

She blows her nose. 'Sorry, love. I'll . . . I'll be home soon. I promise. Be good for Pat.'

'Mum?' She's crying, I know she is! 'MUM!'

'Take care, sweetheart . . . I'll be back soon . . . '

The phone goes dead.

Pat takes the phone, listens, frowns. She moves up the settee to make room for me. 'Come and sit here, Mikey. Don't worry. Gran's looking after her—best place for her.'

I squash next to her. It's so tidy now that it doesn't feel right to put my feet on the coffee table.

'Really?'

'Yes, *really*.' Pat smiles. 'She'll be as right as rain soon. What say we watch TV? I just fancy slobbing out. I'm pooped.'

I remember Meg and the 'poopy-doo'. I smile back.

She hands me the remote control. 'You choose, Mikey.'

I flick the channels till I find *The Simpsons*. We stay like that for ages, sitting next to each other watching TV. Pat keeps smiling at me and saying what fun it is but it feels weird that Mum isn't here. I keep thinking she's going to walk in from the kitchen with a bottle of beer, but she never does.

I still feel weird when I go to bed. Something is wrong but I don't know what. I stand for ages with the lights off, looking down the garden at the shed. It's black-as-black but it's watching me back.

I know you're in there somewhere, Dad. Come out and help Mum come home. She's not OK but I don't know what to do. Come back and help me. You listening? Even if you've done something bad, you've got to help.

The wind shakes the windows. The trees bend and shiver. I'm glad Timmer is right next to me, curled up on the floor. I crawl into bed and watch the shadows dance on the wall as I fall asleep.

It takes a minute for me to realize that it's Timmer scratching at me. I'm all sweaty. There's no breeze coming in the window. It's so hot. I was fast asleep but I can't quite remember my dream. I think it was to do with the little calf—she kept wanting and wanting something from me but I didn't understand what. I close my eyes and try to find her.

Timmer paws at me and whines.

What is it, boy? It's still the middle of the night and I'm tired!

He whines again and pushes his wet nose under my arm. I sit up and rub my eyes. The street-light is shining through my bedroom window. The orange curtains haven't shut properly so I can see the house opposite. It's dark but they haven't shut the curtains. I don't like that.

The house looks like it's got black eyes and they're watching me. Timmer is watching me too. He looks towards the window and growls and walks towards my bed, ears back.

What's out there, Tims?

The duvet is all twisty and it takes a minute to get it off me. I stumble as I get out of bed and stub my toe on the bedside table. I yelp. It bloody hurts. I'm all muddly and it's the middle of the night, Timmer-dog! This better be worth it. I limp to the window. I pull back the curtains. My hand stops. The curtains are cold. Very cold. Crackly. Almost frosty.

I go very still. It feels like something is here in the room with me. Timmer is right next to me but not just him. Something else. I turn slowly. Nothing I can see— just my furniture, the mess on the floor, the shadows . . . What is it?

My back is to the window and the staring house and I spin round quick.

The house-face looks back at me. *And?* it says, *what do you want, Mikey Mikey? The boy who can't work anything out. The boy whose father has gone away. Heh? Heh?*

Nothing.

Or is there?

Just out of the corner of my eye, I see something down the road to my right. *A flash of bright something.* I shiver. It looks familiar but I don't know why. Everything dark is alive out there. It's all watching me. All of it. Waiting.

Another flash. Smoke is wriggling up into the night sky.

Is this more of the stuff that Cackler said would make things better? I go still. My neck prickles. Someone *is* here in my room. I turn and stare into the dark. The dark stares back.

'Dad?'

I stand, waiting for an answer.

Nothing.

The clock on the landing chimes. The frost crackles at the window. Whatever is out there is calling me. The dark in the bedroom presses against me, pushing me into the night.

'You want me to see something out there?' I whisper.

Timmer whines and scratches at the door. I bend down to pull on my trainers.

Coming, doggie, I'm coming. I wait just a bit longer with my hand on the door handle. Still silence. Pat snores, dead to the world as I slip down the stairs and into the street.

All the shadows line up in the window of the house-face eyes as I walk past but I don't look at them. I keep going. A white sparkly path is growing in front of me, stretching along the middle of the road into the distance. Everything is quiet. It's like a ghost-town in the films and I am the only survivor. It's hot but there's no breeze. I'm at the edge of the circle of light from the street-lamp now. I have to walk in the dark a bit before I get to the light-circle of the next one. Timmer is next to me. I rub just between his ears. I couldn't do this without you, mate. I couldn't.

There's more smoke now, going up up up into the night sky. It's hissing my name to the stars. The bright is just round the corner of the road.

I'll see it in a minute.

It's not a still bright—it's a bright light that's moving.

I get closer. It knows I'm coming. Just a bit further now. I pass Albert's house. I pass the newsagent's on the corner. Timmer's claws click on the pavement, telling me it's all right and I'm safe when he's with me.

I put my hand on his head when we get to the corner of the road.

This is it.

It's the garage where Dad used to work back when the buildings and stuff were still here. It's on fire.

My head is muzzy. I never come here. I rub my eyes. Am I really out in the dark night in front of this Backwards fire?

It's the night the garage burned down. Not like little fireplace flames—big monster eat-everything-up flames, a great wall of them.

It's so hot I'm nearly blasted to the other side of the street. Behind me, I can hear the Backwards people coming to watch. I can't take my eyes off the flames though. **They are alive and angry and strong. They snap** like teeth and dance a jerky dance. They hide behind beams and barrels and then you realize there's loads of 'em, just building up their strength to go mental and burn burn burn. I can't stop watching.

There's a loud crash and part of the roof falls in. A black cloud rushes out. Far away, I hear the sirens of the fire-engines. The fire is so hot that, even though the Backwards people are starting to fade, my skin burns.

We're going further Backwards, though. The world is swirling again. It makes my eyes sting. The fire is getting younger, littler. The building isn't so burnt.

I am on my own with Timmer.

Almost.

Someone is standing in the shadows just around the corner of the building. Even though my skin is hot, there's ice in my belly. I want to leave now, Timmer, but I can't. I can't move my feet. I have to watch. This bit of Backwards is just for me.

The fire is a baby-fire; it's nearly back to before it started. It's the dead of night. Silent all around. There is a sizzly noise and the fire is gone. The garage is new again and the world is asleep.

The man comes out of the dark.

He's dressed in black and still in the shade but I know him. I know him. I know him. He's leaning to one side because he's carrying a plastic can and it's heavy. He walks to the front of the garage and stands, back to me, just for a moment.

I could hear a pin drop. I lean forwards to watch. This is important but I don't know why. Timmer, what's happening?

Timmer sits down. He licks my hand. He's telling me I'm all right. I'm all right.

I look up. **Dad is on the move.**

He walks across the car park in front of the garage. He is a bit slow; he's nervous. The moon is bright for a moment. He stops, turns round. He's frowning and biting his lip.

I want to run over to him. I want him to smile when he sees me and ruffle my hair and take me home. I want him to walk in the door and call to Mum and hug her and make her eyes shine.

The clouds cover the moon again and it's dark. Dad turns back to face the garage. He takes a deep breath as he walks towards the side door.

C'mon, Timmer, let's follow him.

His shoes are quiet but he jangles in his pocket as he pulls out some keys. The lock clicks. The door swings open.

It smells of oil and petrol in here. I can almost taste it. Dad bends down to undo the petrol can. I watch his hands, black fingernails and chunky fingers. Petrol sloshes out onto the floor.

There's a bobble in my throat. Timmer sniffs the concrete.

There are three cars in here but one of them is in bits

all over the floor. They're in hospital, all lined up ready to be made better. Dad walks round them, sloshing all over the place. There's a calendar next to me. There's a naked woman on it—all curvy and smiley and soft. Ralph's naked curvy woman. She's holding a spanner and leaning against a black sports car.

My eyes sting from the petrol and I can't see her properly any more.

Dad stands next to me. He's finished with the can. He wipes the handle with a cloth and then chucks it in the corner and runs his hand across his face and leaves black smudges. He's frowning again.

He reaches inside his shirt pocket and pulls out a box of matches. He turns it round and round on his palm, running his fingers down the sides. He bites his lip. His nails are so short the skin puffs up over the top and the skin is bitten away down the sides of his nails.

I can't stop looking at his hands. They used to tie a shoelace round the arm of the chair for me—over and over again—to teach me how to tie up my shoes, they mended things, ruffled my hair, held Mum's hand.

He pushes the box open and takes out a match. He lights it and holds it out in front of him. Little shadows wriggle on his face. He looks so sad. Gently, he blows it out.

I step closer to him. Just one step.

Dad doesn't move. He shakes his head and his arms drop down to his sides.

I take another step closer. I can smell his Dad-smell now—his soap, his aftershave, the garage-stuff, the underneath Dad too.

He walks back to the garage door slowly. He runs his hands through his hair so it all sticks up. He stops. He turns. His face is twisted.

'C'mon, Stuart, lad!' He is talking to himself but his teeth are clenched together. He punches his own arm. 'C'MON, Stuart!' He hits himself again. 'C'MON!'

The shadows are waking up. I can hear them rustling all around the garage. I pull Timmer close. He whines quietly but stays near me.

Dad takes the matches out of his pocket again. He strikes one. This match is stronger than the first one. I can hear it hissing. This flame is bad. It's hungry.

Everyone watches it fall. Dad. Me. Timmer. We all hold our breath.

The flame moves like a curvy naked woman dancing. There are lots of flames all across the floor. A moving swirly carpet of fire. It looks beautiful.

I stand watching.

Flames are eating each car now, moving up the wooden benches at the back, a piece of paper on the floor burns bright bright bright . . .

There's a smashing noise behind me. Dad has picked up a crowbar and broken the window in the door from the other side. The glass is all over the floor.

I want to stay close to Dad. It crunches like crisps under my shoes as I follow him out.

He waits, just for a moment, looking back at the garage. Half his face is bright from the street-light, and half is in the dark. His eyes are flashing but now I'm up close, I can't tell if he's angry or going to cry. His shoulders heave up: he cries like a hurt animal.

Then he's running running running into the night.

Timmer and me watch him go. We don't move.

Behind me, I can feel the heat of the fire on my back as it gets stronger and stronger and stronger.

Chapter Seventeen

My duvet is tangled as usual. I can't move when I wake up. I wriggle until I can sit up. Did I really see the burning in the Backwards last night? Timmer opens one eye and looks at me. I'm still wearing my trainers: it must be true.

I stand up too quickly to look out the window. Little stars twinkle all around the room. The shadows are getting darker around the shed. He's in there watching me even though I can't see him. Dad did the burning but he didn't want to do it. And then they caught him in the woods but it wasn't right. My head starts to ache. I hold on to the windowsill. The Backwards is telling me a story and it makes me feel dizzy. I wonder if the shadows will be quieter at the garage now that I've seen its bad Backwards like in Little Mikey's room. I shiver—those flames were hot and strong and dangerous.

Albert is in his garden next door. He's just finished trimming his hedge. Even from here, I can see his smile. He loves making things neat and tidy. Everything in his garden is in rows and all his plants are extra-bright and happy. Our garden isn't like that. We haven't got a proper lawn—the grass is in lumps and there are empty bits where Timmer and me scuff the football.

Boys are playing in the scrubland-before-the-fields—not the lads, just other boys. That makes me jump. The lads. Dave. I'm supposed to find out when he's going to the pub to tell Ralph. Then Ralph will help me find Dad. Then . . . then . . .

Come on, Timmer, let's go go go!

Pat grabs my arm as we run through the kitchen. 'Where are you off to in such a hurry?'

'I'm doing an errand for Cackler's man. I promised.' I wriggle free.

'Not without breakfast first, you're not.' She pushes my shoulders down so I sit at the table and she passes me a plate of toast. As I stuff it down, she gives Timmer his morning biscuits.

I wrinkle my nose. Timmer's my dog, not hers! I feed him. It's my job!

'I loved watching TV with you last night, Mikey. It's nice to have some company.' Pat smiles at me.

I crunch my toast hard. I want her to leave me alone.

'Fancy meeting up after this errand of yours? We could go into town, do a bit of shopping together.'

My belly squeezes. 'I don't like shops.' They're too busy—make me muddled, make my head black.

'Yes, yes.' Pat's neck goes pink. 'I forgot. You're an outdoors boy, aren't you?'

I nod. I stand up. I want to go out quick before she thinks of something else. Pat follows me to the door but I just keep going.

Me and Timmer walk up the street together. Where am I going to find Dave, Timmer? I don't know where the lads hang out because I don't hang out with anyone, except you and now Ralph. It's bloody boiling today. It's all shivery above the road, called mirrors or something, Mum said.

Timmer's tongue is hanging out. Maybe the lads are nearby, Timmer-dog and we don't need to go too far. We've got to keep looking though because Ralph is finding Dad so we have to do our bit too. Like we promised.

'All right, Michael?' Albert is in his front garden now, pulling the dead pink petals off the roses. 'These were beauties, these roses. Did you see them?'

I smile. I can't remember. Timmer snuffles against his legs, wagging his tail hard.

'Yes, now it's time for the chrysanthemums.' He runs his hand gently over the yellow twiddly petals. 'We all have our turn to bloom, don't we?'

'Yes, Albert.'

'What are you up to on this fine day?'

'Trying to find the lads. Y'know, Toby and Jim and Dave. Seen 'em?'

Albert frowns. 'Not your sort, are they? They were in the bus-shelter when I went to buy my paper a little while ago.' He looks at me for a second. 'You be careful, won't you, lad?'

I give him a big smile so he stops worrying. 'OK, Albert.'

I walk towards the bus-shelter from behind so I can see inside through the glass. We go slowly. Timmer is panting because it's so hot. There are two people standing there with their backs to me. I can't see them properly. The lads? I click my fingers so Timmer comes close—it's too hot to hold his fur. A little bit closer. I still can't see who they are but I'm starting to taste an icy wind.

The people are bigger than the lads. They're men, facing each other and clenching their fists. The men get clearer . . . one is small, fat, with a big hat, the tramp, and the other one is tall and has dark hair like Dad . . .

I squeeze my eyes shut. I don't want to see. I don't want to know about Dad and the tramp.

'Stay away,' I whisper. 'Just stay away.'

'OI!' someone shouts from behind. 'Who are you talking to?'

I turn round. It's the lads. They've come back! They're grinning at me. Are they my mates or not, Timmer? Jim steps forward.

'You off in la-la land again, Mikey Mikey?'

He nods towards the corner of the bus-shelter where the tramp used to live. I look over. Timmer sniffs it a bit, then wanders off. The bus-shelter is empty.

'Do you see them sometimes too?' I say.

Toby is at Jim's elbow, leaning on him. Jim frowns until he steps away again.

'Did I see who, Mikey-baby?' They both smile twisty smiles and step forwards. They're too close to me. I dig my fingers into my arm. Dave hangs back.

'The Backwards people! Did you see them?' I ask.

'Yeah, course we did, Mikey!' Toby says.

The lads all laugh. I laugh too but I'm not sure.

There's a grey stray dog walking this way. Timmer stands straight, staring at it. Easy, Timmer! Easy, boy! The grey dog comes closer, stands still. Timmer goes up to it slowly, slowly, then sniffs its bum. The grey dog circles, does the same to Timmer. It's all right. I breathe out. They're friends now.

'Hey, look over there!' says Jim, pointing to the red roof on the house opposite the bus-shelter. 'See him, Mikey?'

'Who?' I can't see anyone. Am I being stupid again?

'Just there, mate!' Jim points to the same place. 'Sitting

up by the chimney!' He snorts and his eyes water when he says that.

I stand up. I can't see anyone. I look at the roof on the house next-door. Nothing. The roof on the other side. Nothing.

Jim shakes his head. 'Ah, Mikey-boy. You're just never going to be able to join our gang if you can't even see straight, now, are you?'

I make my fingers go stiff. I look really hard. *Where* do they mean? Why can't I see it? I'm so stupid. SO STUPID! I can't see anything but red tiles on an empty roof.

Toby laughs. 'Try a bit harder, won't you, Mikey-boy?'

I clench my teeth and stare and stare and stare. 'Who is it up there?'

Jim slaps me on the back. He shakes as he splutters out 'Santa Claus, mate.' The lads burst out laughing. Timmer jumps.

I've done something wrong. I didn't get the joke. Could they see the Backwards?

'I thought you wanted to be my mate,' I say.

'Yeah but you keep failing all our . . . simple . . . little . . . tests, don't you?' Jim taps me on the head hard when he says 'simple' and 'little' and 'tests'.

It's true. I messed up the drinking test and Ralph had to save me. Ralph? Ralph! I am supposed to be finding out about Dave. I hit my head with my hand. I nearly bloody forgot!

169

'When are you going to the Horse and Hounds again?'
I say. 'Tonight?'

Toby rubs his hands together and hooks his arm round
Jim's shoulders. Dave sighs and looks the other way.

'Persistent little fella, ain't he?' says Toby.

Dave whispers something to Jim but he ignores him.

'Good for a laugh though. You still want to join our
gang, Mikey?' Jim says.

He hooks his arm round Toby's shoulder and they
both lean forwards. Dave is standing behind them. They
look so cool and old.

'Yeah!' Well, I *think* I do but not if it was like last
time.

'Tonight it is then. Horse and Hounds. Be prepared
for your next test, Mikey-baby.' Jim punches my arm. It
hurts. I don't want another test.

'Dave's coming too?' I look over at him.

He pushes his hands into his pockets and kicks the
edge of the pavement. 'Yes, Mikey. I'll be there too.'

Dave turns round and walks away from the bus-shelter
down the road towards the little precinct. Jim and Toby
look at each other and Toby says something I can't hear.
I hop from one foot to the other. Whispering I can't hear
makes me squirmy.

'Laters, Mikey!' Jim does a high-five with me but I
miss. He rolls his eyes. My face burns. He walks away
with Toby.

I look back at the bus-shelter. It's empty but the cold is biting again. Frost crackles across the glass. The Backwards is still there, waiting for me—this strange Backwards with the frost in it. I take a step away. I don't want to see it but I'm the only one that *can* see it—the lads couldn't. That makes me feel heavy. Cackler is the only one who understands it. Cackler and maybe Meg.

Let's go home, now, Timmer. We can tell Ralph about Dave going to the pub.

'Tonight you say, Mikey, at the Horse and Hounds?' Ralph hoses down the udders on the last cow in the milking stand.

'Yes.'

The cow stamps her hooves. This one doesn't like being shut in the milking stall so they do her last so she gets out quick. Ralph pulls the lever and the little gate thing lifts up. The cow lets out a low moo and pushes out.

'Easy there, girl, eeeeeeeasy there.' Ralph slaps her back as she goes by. The cow moves a bit faster and rushes straight out of the barn. Ralph wipes his forehead with his sleeve.

'Well done, Mikey. Well done. That's really quick work.' He flashes me a big smile. 'Big help, ta.'

My chest goes big and puffy. I did well. I'm doing mate-things. We walk outside into the sunshine.

'What time shall we go, Ralph?'

Ralph stops and puts his hand on my shoulder. 'Go where, mate?'

'To the pub?'

He puts his head on one side and doesn't say anything.

'You know, the Horse and Hounds where we're going to meet up with Dave and Toby and Jim.' I bend my legs up and down a bit. 'The lads. I'm doing another test to be part of their gang.'

'Ah, don't think that's a good idea, Mikey. Perhaps best if you don't come along this time.'

'Why not?'

Ralph pats my back. 'It's boring, mate. Won't be there long anyways. I'll tell them you said you'd see them another time. Much better if we do something more interesting together. What do you say?'

He smiles and the shadows start to chatter.

'Do what?'

'I dunno. Fishing maybe. Or something . . . '

'Let's go to the beach!'

Ralph yawns. 'Sure, maybe the beach if you like.'

Fizzes whizz down my legs and I do my bendy-legs some more. Ralph raises an eyebrow and starts to walk across the yard. The gravel crunches.

'Did you find out about Dad?'

Ralph stops. 'I did, mate. You were right, he ain't at the

prison any more.' He bites his lip. 'Has your mum talked to you about him?'

I shake my head. 'Mum's staying at Gran's—she's not well.'

My eyes sting and so I turn and watch the cows walking out the gate and into the field. My eyes are blurry though and I can't see them properly.

Ralph's watching me out the corner of his eye very carefully. 'I'm sorry, Mikey. I'll keep asking around though, see what I can find out about your dad.' He pats me on my shoulder.

'Oh OK. Thanks.'

Ralph nods and walks after the cows to close the gate. I remember Dad crying like an animal and running into the dark after the burning last night. I shiver. Timmer yaps and runs forward. He's seen someone.

'Hey, boy, you're here again!'

It's Meg. She's carrying a pile of plastic sacks and walking towards me. She's wearing a tight T-shirt with blue writing on.

'Mikey!' She puts the bags down. Big smile. 'Gramps said you were amazing when you found Bess's calf! Hidden in Maitley's Dell!'

I smile.

'How on earth did you find her?'

My belly squeezes. I can't tell her about the Backwards. She'll think I'm weird. 'I sort of followed her . . . '

'How? Her tracks?'

'Kind of . . .'

Meg leans closer. If she leans any more, she'll be touching me. 'What do you mean? Gramps said you're really clever with animal things.'

'Did he?' I can't stop smiling.

Ralph coughs nearby. Makes me jump. I turn round. He's walking back towards the shed—winks at me, nods towards Meg, taps the side of his nose. My face burns.

Did Meg see that big wink from Ralph? I lean from one foot to the other. She looks over my shoulder at him.

'You're getting to be good pals with Ralph, aren't you?'

'Yes, he's my mate.'

I rub my hands together like Ralph does. Meg frowns.

'He's helping me.' I can't tell her about Dad because of the Golden Rule. My hands are going all sweaty and I run them down my T-shirt.

A curl of hair falls over Meg's face—twirls of hair in front of freckles. 'How is he helping you, Mikey?'

'He's helping me find someone.'

'Who?' Her eyes go big.

The curl of hair blows in the wind. I hear water whooshing out of a tap in the shed, before the door swings shut.

'I can't tell you,' I whisper.

'Oh, OK.' She looks down at the ground.

Timmer's watching me with sad eyes. It's no good, Timmer-dog. Mum has said loads of times I can't talk about Dad. I mustn't!

'I promised.' I can hardly hear myself, I'm so quiet.

Meg shrugs. 'Be careful, Mikey. Be careful.'

'Why? Aren't you friends with Ralph?'

Meg chews her lip. 'Ralph just works on Gramps's farm, Mikey. That doesn't mean he's my friend.' She waits. 'I'm just worried about you, that's all.'

I twist the end of my belt round my hand. I pull it tight. What is she saying?

'Ralph's helped me before. He's my mate.'

Meg's face snaps shut. She pats Timmer on the head, then picks up the pile of bags again. 'Up to you, Mikey.' They slip a bit so she lifts her knee up and rests them on it while she gets a better hold. 'I'd better get on.'

'Are you still friends with me, Meg? I can't tell you about it—I promised. Ralph's not a bad 'un, is he?'

Meg shrugs her shoulders. 'Like I said, just be careful, Mikey.' She walks off across the yard and doesn't look back.

Chapter Eighteen

I stand watching her walking away. She doesn't turn round, just keeps on going. She didn't say she was still my friend. She didn't smile. All the happy-all-right-feeling in me is going down and down me, through my feet and into the ground, like water going into the soil. Meg still hasn't looked back at me to say 'goodbye'.

I lean on one foot and then the other. Timmer is sniffing in the grass by the gatepost. What did I do wrong, Timmerdog? I was only helping Ralph out. High up the hills, there are the cows—all my friends like Old Mary and Bess and the calves. Meg was with me up there. Meg and me.

A tractor starts in the yard behind the sheds—Ralph is on the move. Meg stumbles. The plastic bags are slipping down again. The bundle is too big for her. One bag slides on to the floor. She nearly falls over.

'I'll help!' I run over to her. Timmer is quicker than me. He's there straight away.

'You're still here!' Meg turns round, surprised. Her hair is all over her face.

My hands are going all sticky. Is that a bad thing? Should I have gone home? I pick up the bag extra-quick.

'Thanks, Mikey!' Her face is a bit red and sweaty and she lets me take the other bags from her. 'They are a funny shape to carry. I just need to put them in that outhouse over there . . . Gramps can sort them out when he comes down from the field . . .'

I walk over with her. She looks up at me and smiles. 'This is sweet of you!' Her freckles look smiley too. She opens the door and points to another pile of bags on the floor. 'Just over there, please.'

'I didn't want you to be mad at me . . .' I drop them down.

Meg's eyes and mouth go wide and round in surprise. 'Oh, Mikey!' She laughs and leans over and gives me a hug. 'I wasn't *mad* at you! I just want to make sure you're OK!'

I'm tingling all over. She gave me a hug! SHE GAVE ME A HUG! Timmer wags his tail and his tongue is lolling out of his mouth. I'm all sunshiney through and through and through. I hug her back tight.

'Hey!!!' She pulls away again. 'You're stronger than you think, Mikey!' She's laughing.

'You're still my friend?'

'Of *course* I am.'

My smile is big and my legs start doing the bendy-leg dance all on their own. Timmer barks to join in.

'Shhhhhh, Timmer! You'll disturb the animals.' Meg grabs his collar. 'Let's go into the garden and have a drink. Come on!' She grins.

I haven't been in the farmhouse garden before. It's different to being in the fields and in the farmyard—it makes me want to be on my best behaviour. I put Timmer on his lead so he's polite too. There's loads of flowers—all different colours—near the house and then there's some grass and then some trees further away and the reeds are behind them.

There's a table with some upside down plastic glasses and some lemonade in a jug with a lid on it. I choose a blue glass and Meg takes a green one. I'm going all fizzy inside because it feels all sort of proper. There's a plastic box with cherries in it too.

'Mmmmmmm, Mum's been picking some cherries from the orchard.' Meg wipes her sleeve across her forehead and picks up the box. ''S too hot. Let's sit in the shade.'

We walk down to the trees and Meg sits under an apple tree. The sunlight through the leaves makes patterns on the ground. Meg leans against the trunk. The light is dancing on her legs and arms and face too now.

'Gramps will be back soon—he's up checking on the calves. There's so much to do this time of year.' She closes her eyes. 'Boy, I'm tired. I've been up since five thirty.'

I swallow the lemonade in big gulps until it's all gone. My tongue is tangy and zingy. I want to say something clever but I feel all big arms and big feet so I eat another cherry instead. Timmer turns round in a circle on some long grass and curls up. Meg still has her eyes closed. I move my foot so it is nearly touching her boot. I waggle my shoe but still don't let it quite touch hers. I want to but I don't. Meg giggles. She's got one eye open now and she's squinting at me. My face is red.

She sits up straight and crosses her legs and drinks some lemonade.

'The reeds are growing well, aren't they?' She nods towards the end of the garden. 'The RSPB man is pleased.'

The grass goes down a bit towards the end of the garden and then the reeds start and go on and on and on.

'Which man?'

Meg smiles. 'The man that comes to talk to Gramps about the bitterns in the reed-bed. Some of the reeds grow on our land, and most are on the reserve land but everyone wants to work together to see if we can get the bitterns to stay. They like big reed beds so Gramps is doing his best to help.'

'Cackler is helping to make a home for the bitterns?' I sit up straight.

Meg nods. 'Yup.'

The reeds are all wavy from here like the sea. They go on for ages—all the way towards the river and then off in the distance. My bittern is in there. Maybe her nest too. I like that the reeds are tall—they will hide her. Cackler is helping her to stay safe.

Meg suddenly laughs. 'What *are* you thinking, Mikey? You look very serious!'

I lean closer. 'I've seen a bittern . . .'

Meg sits up tall. Her eyebrows go up. 'Have you?! That's not fair! I spend all my time on this farm and I've never seen one! I've only heard the males booming, same as everyone else . . .'

I puff out my chest a bit. 'Me and her fish together sometimes.'

Meg's eyes are wide. 'Wow, Mikey! Even the RSPB man has never seen one near here—he could only count them by recording the males booming—and then he guesses how many females might be here too.'

I'm so smiley my cheeks ache. Even the special bird-man hasn't seen a bittern here! I hug my knees tight and tap my toes on the grass. I look at her. I can't believe that Meg is sitting here talking to me about bitterns. I throw a cherry up in the sky and catch it in my mouth. Ta daaaaa! No hands! My party trick.

Meg laughs and claps at me. She's gone all sparkly. I smile hard hard hard at her and she laughs again. Then I go all whizzy and stuff masses of cherries in my mouth all at once. Just squish them in. I look over at her. She doesn't laugh though, the way they would at school. She's frowning a bit. I am just about to open my mouth to show all the cherry mush but then I stop. I don't think she'd laugh about that either.

I sort of hold my hand over my mouth as I start to chew.

Meg looks away and picks up her lemonade. 'The RSPB man says there's only one male bittern here though at the moment. There's a nice story about that . . . ' Meg says, taking a swig. 'The sound of the male birds is like a fingerprint—you can tell which bird it is from the noise it makes.'

I can't open my mouth because of all the cherries in there. I wipe my chin with my sleeve. There's loads of juice and it's spilling out a bit.

Meg wrinkles up her nose. 'Mikey!'

I shrug a sorry.

Meg puts her glass down. 'Anyhow, the RSPB man said that when they listened to the sounds of our reed-bed they had a nice surprise . . . '

'What was it?' I take a couple of cherry stones out of my mouth and put them on the grass. I can talk better now. 'What was the surprise?'

Meg smiles and lifts her shoulders up like she's all scrunchy and happy. 'They played back the recording and guess what?'

'What?'

'They recognized the voice of the bittern! They'd recorded it before—he lived on another nature reserve and then he just disappeared. No one knew where he had gone, they thought perhaps he was dead . . .'

'But he wasn't?'

'No! He came to this reed bed!'

'Wow!' I stroke Timmer's ears. 'He just wanted to live somewhere else. He wanted to live here.'

Meg smiles. 'Maybe you saw him by the river. It's hard to tell the males and females apart you know.'

I shake my head. 'No, I think my bittern's a she-bittern. I reckon she has a nest.'

Meg chews slowly on another cherry. 'Maybe, but you'd never find a nest if she has. She'd make it right in the middle of the reed bed where no one can find it. The RSPB man said the first time you would see the fledglings is when they start to fly.'

There's a clink of the gate behind us. Cackler is standing there, waving at us. I wave back. Cackler smiles and shouts across at us. 'Hello, Mikey! Five minutes, Meg, then I'll run you home . . .' He waves again and wanders into the house.

Meg yawns and picks up the empty glasses. 'Time for me to go now, Mikey.'

I stand up with her and we walk back towards the house. Ralph is in the distance, driving the tractor back to the farm. I don't want him to see me here with Meg. I like it that it was just us chatting today.

'Thanks for the lemonade and cherries, Meg.' I want to be proper and polite.

'Maybe you can show me where you saw the bittern some time?'

I punch the air. 'YESSSS!!!'

Meg laughs. Curls and freckles. 'See you back here soon then?'

'YES!' Timmer barks when I say that. 'Soooooooon!!' I sing as I run down towards the farm gate and up the hill on the other side. Timmer runs next to me. My legs are excited and want to run for ever.

The reeds whisper down the hill near the river. They go on for miles and miles. Maybe the bitterns are in there, hiding and watching me. I slow down. I look back and see that Ralph has driven the tractor back into the farmyard and jumps down. It seems ages ago since we had our chat this afternoon. He said that I was right, that Dad isn't in prison any more.

I turn away from him and walk down the path towards the quiet of the river. I don't want to run any more. Inside I feel very soft and when I talk to Timmer, my voice hardly makes a noise at all. 'Did you hear what Meg said, Timmer-dog? They thought the Dad-bittern was gone for ever but he wasn't. He came back here. He's secretly living in there, near our bittern probably. He wasn't dead or lost after all.'

Chapter Nineteen

The birds are dancing in the sky when I get back to the river. Loads of them, all together. Dancing—this way, then that way—like a shoal of fish. The sky is big above the fields and the river. Big and blue. This is the end-of-day-bird-dance. I stand and watch it for ages. It makes my head all gentle and wide at the same time.

This is near where I met Ralph. He isn't a bad 'un. I know he's not. He's helped me with the lads. We had lunch together. He showed me the animals on the farm. He's finding Dad for me. Why doesn't Meg like him? I take in a deep breath so I go all big and puffy and then, whoosh, let it out again. If I do this lots of times it makes my head nice and dizzy.

I look around for my bittern. I haven't seen her for ages. I feel bad about that. Grey-cloud-sad in my head.

Let's go and see her, Timmer. Let's go now before we go home. We might even see the Dad-bittern too.

I walk ever so slowly up the riverbank because I have to look really carefully. She's shy, my bittern. She can stand right in front of you, head pointed tall to the sky, but she's so still that sometimes you can't see her. Timmer is running far away up the river, chasing seagulls that have landed there. I don't think he'll bother her today.

I get to my fishing spot and sit down. The river makes me quiet. It's moving fast. I throw a stick onto the water and watch it float away. The sun is going down and it shines on the water. Sun on water. Beautiful.

I look in the reeds for my bittern but can't see her. I wonder if she came here before the Dad-bittern. Or maybe she followed him. Or maybe they came together.

I chew my lip. Could I use the Backwards to find her like I did the missing calf or Prison Officer Jane Smith's name? I know the answer to that: I couldn't because the bittern doesn't want me to know. It's her quiet everyday life and she likes to be hidden. The riverbank would keep her secrets for her.

I close my eyes and feel the river in front of me, like it's been here for ever. The Backwards has been here for ever too, running underneath everything, but I think sometimes its secrets are too big and too strong and they spill out in puddles for me to see.

The shoal of birds is still dancing in the sky. I lean back so the sun is on my face. Cackler said that seeing those puddles of Backwards is a gift. When I watched the Backwards in Little Mikey's room, it made the shadows quieter.

The morning star is out already—that means the moon will be out soon too. The wind blows my hair.

I pick a dandelion head from the grasses. A dandelion clock. I blow it to see how many puffs it takes for the hair-stuff to come off. One, two, three o'clock. The dandelion hair floats on the wind, lands on the river and gets pulled downstream. It gets stuck in the roots of the willow tree. This is another place where the shadows are loud. This is the place I never fish. I stand up and walk over the bridge towards it on the other side of the river. Slowly though.

Not too close.

Not yet.

A wind whispers in its leaves. The sunlight still dances on the water. I take a step closer. This place has shadows, but not really dark ones like where the tramp died. I lean in further—far away someone is laughing, laughing in the Backwards here. A boy. A young boy. I take another step forward. The world swirls.

Little Mikey laughs again. He's sitting by the river on the willow roots. He's opened the plastic box of maggots. They wriggle and squirm. Little Mikey puts his fingers in them.

'Uggggggh!' he squeals and laughs. 'They are disguuuuusting!' He puts his other fingers in and wiggles them around.

'OH, MIKEY!'

I jump like someone's just hit me.

It's Dad. He's sitting the other side of me. 'Take your hands out that box! How many times? . . . '

I turn round.

Dad's shaking his head but his eyes are smiley. He's fishing but he's watching Little Mikey too out the corner of his eye.

'Ahhhhhh!' Little Mikey puts his head on one side like Timmer does when he's doing his hungry face. 'Pleeeeeeeease, Dad—just let me hook up another one?'

He can speak quicker than me, Little Mikey can. There's a bobble in my throat and it won't go down. I remember now: when I was Little Mikey, I loved fishing with Dad. I try to swallow again. I really loved it.

Dad shakes his head but he's grinning. He balances his rod between two rocks and goes over to Little Mikey, giving a pretend-big sigh. 'Just one more, Mikey, but you'll have to go into the field to play when my friend arrives. OK?'

Little Mikey grins as Dad reaches for his fishing rod, then leans against Dad's shoulder. Dad pulls out a maggot from the box. It's little in his big fingers. Little Mikey puts his arms around Dad's neck to watch closer. Dad stops, turns to Little Mikey and kisses his cheek like he can't help it.

'Hey, what's that?' Dad picks his nose. 'Urgh! Mikey, look! Look what I found!' He pretends to pull the maggot out of his nose.

Little Mikey squeals and punches Dad's arm. 'Maggot bogey! Maggot bogey!!!'

They both snort because they're laughing so hard and Little Mikey stamps his feet. The wind blows in the branches of the willow tree and the leaves sigh. Little Mikey looks up and smiles at Dad and Dad looks down and smiles at Little Mikey. Dark curly hair and blond curly hair. Dad and Little Mikey. Little Mikey and Dad.

I want to put my arms round them so we're all a big circle together but I can't—I'm far away in the Now.

'Having fun, you two?'

We both jump and turn round. A man is standing behind the tree. Neither of us heard him coming.

I take a big breath when I see who it is.

It's the other man in the photo with Ralph and Dad at the garage. He's wearing blue overalls today, all dirty with oil stains. He comes and sits next to Dad, leaning back on his hands. Frost crackles out across the grass when he sits down.

I know him, I know I do. I look at his face—*those blue eyes, that big squishy nose*. Who is he? I pull my knees up and hug them close. The cold bites my fingers.

'We'll finish this later, there's a good lad, Mikey. Now run off for five minutes, will yer?'

Little Mikey stands up and smiles at the men, then pulls a football out of the fishing bag and kicks it out into the field. The men watch him run after it.

'So, tonight's the night then, Stuart.' The man smiles at Dad. 'You all right with it all? Ready to go?'

Dad picks up his rod and casts the line back in.

I look around for the bittern but she doesn't belong in this Backwards.

The shoal of birds is still dancing in the sky though. Dad watches them for a minute, then licks his lips.

'You're gonna make it right with me, en't you, Bill?'

'Of course. I told you. Meet me in the woods afterwards and I'll get you out of here quick,' says the man quietly.

'And the money?'

'I'll see you right, trust me. I know what this means to you and yours. I'll give it to you myself, mate.'

Dad doesn't say anything. He stares into the water for a long time. The man waits without saying anything too. The river hears it all but keeps on floating by. I hear Little Mikey running in the field behind me.

Timmer runs along beside him.

'It'll make all the difference to you and your missus, Stuart, and that lad of yours too. Just think what you could do with the cash.'

Dad bites his lip.

'You're not having second thoughts now, are you? You know I'll see you right here, don't you?'

The man leans over and puts a hand on Dad's arm. He and Dad look at each other for a moment. The man smiles. Dad relaxes and smiles back.

'Yes, of course. Just nervous that's all.'

'Good man.' The man pats him on the back. 'We'll have the party to end all parties when it's over. You're my right hand man. Best of the bunch.'

Dad laughs.

'Any worries, let me know. Otherwise, see you in the woods tonight.' The man puffs a bit as he stands up.

Dad doesn't get up. He rubs his finger along the fishing rod gently. His hand is shaking.

'See you later, Bill,' he says softly.

The man walks away. I watch him as he moves along the riverbank. He has an upsy-downsy walk and his right foot isn't working properly. I hadn't noticed that before.

Dad pulls out a cigarette from his shirt pocket and lights up. He turns and watches Little Mikey doing karate kicks. His eyes are watery. He puffs on the cigarette and then he whispers like he's got some gurgles in his throat.

'I'm doing this for you, Mikey-boy. For you and me and Mum.'

The wind blows the cigarette smoke in front of his face so I can't see him properly for a minute. I know what he's doing though. He's hiding behind it, hiding like my bittern.

Behind me, Bill is walking away.

I wrap the edge of my T-shirt round my hands, unwrap, wrap, unwrap. I can't keep still. This is Bill, the man that Dad was looking for in the woods when the black-and-whites came for him. My head is going black. I grit my teeth. I want to scream at Dad, to yell in his face, but he can't hear me in the Backwards. He can't hear me. I pull my hair. I hit my legs. I kick the grass hard hard hard.

He doesn't come for you, Dad! It all goes wrong!

Bill is lying.

HE'S BLOODY LYING!

Chapter Twenty

Dad did it for us. That's what he just said. He did the burning for Mum and me so we had some more money.

There are thunderclouds swirling in my head as I walk home. Was Dad a bit of a good 'un as well? Even though he went to prison? Even though he might have killed the tramp? I groan. I want to stop him, tell him not to go. I pull my hair HARD. I can't change the Backwards—Dad does the burning, he gets caught in the woods, he leaves Mum and me—so what can I do? WHAT CAN I DO?

Behind my eyes aches like I've eaten too much ice-cream. I shake my head to try to make it clean but it's still all messy with black clouds.

I want to talk to Mum. But she's not here. Nobody is in the right bloody place, are they?

The sun has nearly gone. The stars are coming out. There's a curvy moon, a sideways smile, in the sky. It's laughing at me. Timmer walks near me. He knows I don't want him far away. We get to the edge of the field, just before the scrubland, and a man behind me shouts. Makes me jump.

'Mikey!'

I spin round. Timmer goes all stiff and snarls. I hold his collar. My hand is shaking. The man's tall. I can't see his face. He's a shadow coming out of the dark and he's waking the shadows up in my head. I see the kicking boots. Big shoulders. My scar aches. It can't be . . .

'Mikey!'

Dad?

He steps forward. I move away. Timmer snaps at him so I have to push back on my heels to stop him. He's strong, Timmer is. Really strong.

'It's me, Ralph!'

I take a deep breath. He laughs.

'Scared you, did I?'

'Where have you been?'

I still can't see his face. He's breathing hard like he's been running.

'Just been to pay our friend Dave a little visit . . . Thanks for your help, Mikey.' Ralph does a little bow. 'Fancy joining me for a drink as you're my mate now?'

See, Meg? I told you Ralph was all right. He's a good

bloke—he wants to take me out for a drink like a proper mate. I need a mate today, after that . . . that stuff at the river.

'That'd be cool! The Horse and Hounds?'

'Nah, been there earlier tonight. Bored with that. I'll pick you up on the corner near the newsagent's and we'll go out to the Lion or something, hey? Try something new? A special thank you for my special mate?'

'Yeah!'

I still can't see his face properly because he's standing with his back to the moon. He pats me on the shoulder.

'See you in half an hour then, Mikey.' He sees Timmer. 'Hah!' Ralph stamps his foot right near Timmer's paw.

Timmer lunges at him and I have to yank him back. Easy, boy, eeeeeeasy, boy. I stare at Ralph. My mouth is open.

'Sorry, Mikey!' Ralph lifts his hands up in a stick-'em-up way. 'I was only trying to play with your dog!'

Timmer growls and I stroke his ear. He didn't mean to upset you, Timmer-dog. It's OK.

'See you later, Mikey?' Ralph waits for me to look up and smile at him, then he turns and disappears back into the black.

Pat's in bed when I get home. She waves at me from under the duvet. She's watching TV *again*. There are loads of sweet-wrappers over the duvet like rainbow snowflakes. She starts to pick them up when I walk in, goes a bit red.

'Hello, stranger! Good day with your pal?'

'Cool! I went to the farm. I'm going out with him again tonight.' I hop from one foot to the other.

'The Cackler friend?' Pat shoves the sweet papers in the bin.

'Yep.' I pick at the fringey edge of the lampshade by the door. I make it swish over my fingers.

'You ought to invite him in for a drink, Mikey. So I can say "Hi".'

I scrunch my fingers together. I don't want Pat to meet Ralph. It's not right. 'He's picking me up outside but maybe next time.' I shuffle a bit. I don't want to talk too much to Pat, but my head can't stop buzzing after today. 'Can I ask you something?'

She sits up, smiles really hard. I take a step back.

'Of course. What is it?'

'You can't change things that have happened can you?'

'Ooooooooooooh, Mikey!' She frowns. 'Have you done something you wish you hadn't?'

'NO! I'm not a bad 'un! I just wish I could change something someone else did.'

She twists a ring on her finger. 'Don't we all, Mikey, don't we all.' She smiles a sad smile at me. 'You can't change things, no. Just learn from their mistakes, Mikey, so you can do better yourself.'

I've knocked the lampshade wonky so I make it straight.

'Do you want to talk about anything?' She looks at me sideways.

I shake my head. 'Nah, ta.'

'Sure?'

I shake my head again.

She yawns. 'I'll stay awake till you get in, so not too late, young man, OK?'

'OK.'

Ralph drives really fast. I open the window so the wind is loud. He's smiling but his eyes are wide and they sparkle but not in a smiley way. He holds the wheel tight and leans forwards.

'I'm the King of the Road, Mikey,' he shouts and revs the engine.

It's a little windy country road. Hedges both sides in the headlights. Twisty corners. I push my feet into the floor. My heart is loud. Timmer whimpers on the back seat. Ralph brakes hard. There's a Volvo in front going really slow.

'The KING of the ROAD!' Ralph jams the gearstick into second and the engine screams as we pull out.

There's no room. A car is coming the other way. Ralph slams his foot down on the accelerator. I sit on my hands. The headlights flash. My teeth ache. We pass the Volvo. The other car brakes. We're back on the right side of the road.

'Woooo hooooo!' Ralph laughs.

The other car honks its horn. I dig my fingers into a hole in the seat under my leg. Ralph punches the roof of the car.

'You OK there, Mikey? White knuckle ride, hey?' He winks.

The sign of the Red Lion flashes in the headlights. We turn off the road. The wheels crunch on the gravel and we stop. My belly is tight.

'Pint of bitter? You're still under age so we'll sit in the garden. OK, mate?'

'OK!'

I clip Timmer's lead on. His ears are flat back and I can see the whites of his eyes. A pint of beer. Like one of the blokes. Ralph's so cool. He's just walked inside the bar. My hands are still shaking.

Timmer and me go round the back to the garden. No one else is sitting outside. I pick a table right at the back. Ralph smiles as he pushes my pint over to me.

'To fun!' He holds his glass up too. We clink.

'To fun!'

Ralph pulls a packet of cigarettes out of his shirt

pocket, offers me one, but I don't smoke, and then lights up. The smell reminds me of Mum and her tissues and all those old photos. I take a long gulp of the beer. It's a proper grown-up taste. I don't like it and it makes my eyes water but I have another go anyway. It tastes better than when the lads made me drink it; like when I drank that beer with Ralph on the farm.

'So how's tricks?' Ralph looks at me over his pint.

'OK.' I take a swig but I'm nervous and I spill some beer down my chin.

Ralph licks his lips and smiles.

We both drink again. I feel like a real man. A real drink.

'Any more problems with the lads then, Mikey?'

I shake my head. No problems at all.

'That's good. I'll sort 'em out for you if you do.'

I drink some more. It's tasting better and better. My legs are going all funny and wobbly. The beer fizzes on my tongue. Ralph laughs. His face is red and shiny. I drink drink drink some more. The shadows in the trees have faces. The table is tilting.

I look up at Ralph. Dad is sitting there. Black T-shirt, rosy face. He smiles at me. The world spins. There's no frost anywhere this time. I don't think this is the Backwards. I think this is coming out of my own head.

'Time to look after yourself a bit, Mikey,' says Dad-Ralph.

His eyes twinkle like they did just as he was going to

tease me when I was a nipper. I nod slowly and I can hear my thoughts scraping against each other as I move. I close my eyes and keep my head still.

'I'm glad you could come out tonight.'

Dad-Ralph reaches out his hand. I flinch. He grins and knuckle-bumps me. My mouth stretches into a smile but my face feels funny.

He takes a swig of beer. 'I was wondering if you fancy doing me a favour. I've just been let down by . . . by . . . someone . . . '

He bends over towards me. I can smell Dad's after-shave. The seam down my scar aches and aches. Dad was let down by someone; it was that man in the woods, Bill.

'Do you like fire, Mikey? You know, bonfires?'

I remember Bonfire Night. I can see the flames. I can see Little Mikey. Hot tomato soup in a mug. Guy Fawkes. Dad, lighting sparklers in the fire.

'I love 'em!' My voice doesn't sound quite like mine.

Dad-Ralph winks at me and leans further forward as if he's going to tell me a very special secret. In my head, I see Little Mikey laughing and drawing circles in the night sky with the sparkler. I hold my breath. I see Little Mikey *inside* me.

'I need a little fire-starter. What do you say?'

Timmer leans against me and I can feel his growls against my leg. I reach down to touch him and his hackles are up. Don't be like that, boy.

'What do you mean?'

'All you need to do is throw a bit of petrol around this place and strike a couple of matches. Will only take a few minutes. Then you leave the rest to me.'

'Eh?'

'Just an empty building, Mikey—no harm to anyone. It'll be fun. Your very own bonfire.'

The world stops swirling and goes very still. I can't hear properly.

'A burning?'

'S'ppose so, if that's what you want to call it.'

Ralph wants me to do a burning. Like Dad. I close my eyes. This is wrong. He leans forwards, taps his fingers on the table. The noise jabs at my head. I open my eyes. He's Dad-Ralph again. The shadowy faces move, come closer.

'I know that it didn't work out for your dad, but he thought it was OK to do a burning, didn't he? That's why he did it. He was a good man, wasn't he?'

I sit on my hands. My head is muddy.

'And you know I'm your mate, don't you? I'll help you and make sure it's all all right. Like with the lads. It'll be different from when your dad did the garage—just like a house-bonfire, that's all.'

I can't change the Backwards—I can't save Dad from the black-and-whites. Maybe I can make it right though, like Pat said. Maybe I can do a special bonfire burning, just for Dad. Bill let Dad down, but Ralph will look after me.

Let it all burn. Smoke. I smell smoke and it's making my eyes water. I take a sip of beer and it fizzes in my throat. I picture Dad, prodding the bonfire with his garden fork—his face is lit up by the flames. He turns and smiles at me because I'm his boy and then he turns away and bends down to light a firework. I picture it all inside me.

Inside, not outside.

'I'll make it worth your while. Bit of pocket money for you. Trip to the beach. What do you say?'

The firework shoots up into the night sky and shatters into a thousand tiny lights, like broken lost stars falling down to earth. Dad-Ralph is looking at me, waiting.

'Yeah!'

The shadow-faces are leery now and they are starting to laugh at me, flashing their white-white teeth. Dad-Ralph leans over and smiles.

'That's my boy.'

Chapter Twenty-One

'How was it, Mikey?' Pat sing-songs out from her room when I get home.

I feel sick. My head is still whizzing around. Timmer stays close.

'Fine.' I hold on to the banisters at the top of the stairs. Mum would kill me if she caught me like this. No drink because of my head. No beer for Mikey. 'I'm going to sleep now though.'

'Did you lock up?'

'Yes!'

'Sweet dreams then, pet.'

There's the click as she turns her light off. Her room is dark now. I flop onto my bed. I don't turn any lights on because of the street lamp outside.

My dreams are all muddled. Smoke. Fire. Dad. Ralph.

Tramp. Swirling and twisting and burning. My mouth is dry. Timmer is close. I can't move. The shadows have legs and they are chasing me. Hot dark hands. Pulling me back, back, back into the shed. My head is thudding. The shiny prison door clangs shut.

I wake up. I'm sweating.

I said I'd help Ralph do a burning last night.

At breakfast, my cornflakes crunch extra-loud in my ears. Dad did one and it wasn't good. But he did it for Mum and me though, didn't he? Didn't he? And Ralph is my mate. He helps me and we went out for a drink last night.

I turn round because I can hear Timmer but when I move it jabs hard in my head behind my eyes. He's carrying Mum's slipper in his mouth, drops it on the kitchen floor. He wants to play. His tail thumps on the floor. I throw it a little way, near the kitchen door by the rubbish. Timmer skids across the floor, brings it back, drops it again. He's slobbered all over it. I don't want to play today, Timmer.

Pat's left a shopping list for me, folded up and tucked under the tortoise ashtray. She'll be at work at the supermarket today. I don't want to pick it up because it's giving me a worry-belly. Mum writes down the words for what she wants but sometimes I get all muddled in front of the shopkeeper so she draws a little picture too. I don't know if Pat will know that. I wish Mum was here. I pick up the bowl and slurp up the rest of the milk. Timmer cocks his head on one side. He's watching me, slipper between his paws. Do you think she'll *really* be coming back soon, Timmer-dog?

He wags his tail. Maybe that's a good sign.

I flick open the list with the end of my spoon. Phew! Pat remembered to do it right. Three big carrots all in a row. A pint of milk. Four cakes with cherries on the top. She's drawn a little picture of me at the bottom of the list—I'm eating one of the cakes on the way home. She did that to make me smile. And because I will eat a cake too; I can't help it.

We'd better go and get the stuff for her, Timmer. Out the front door today. Walks later. I pick up the list and the keys and Timmer's lead. Time to go.

The dustbin men are collecting rubbish in the street. Big Rick is picking up the bags outside our house. He used to be at my special school until last year.

'Hi there, Mikey!' He swings three big bags over his shoulder like they are feathers and smiles at me.

'You've lost some teeth!' There's a gap in his mouth at the front.

He grins even harder. 'Too much fighting, Mikey-Mikey!'

The back of the lorry yawns and he chucks the bags in.

'See you around. Don't get into trouble will you?'

The dustbin lorry moves away. *Will* I get into trouble, Timmer? Big Rick winks and picks up the next bags.

'Seeeeeee yooooouuuuuu!' I sing song to him.

'Seeeeeee yooooouuuuuu,' sing songs someone behind me.

I turn round. It's Toby and Jim. 'Seeeeeeeeeee you soooooooooooon, Mikey. Seeeeeeeeee you sooooooooooon.' Then a burst of laughter.

'That one of your pals from the Slooooooooooooow Schooooooool?'

Jim does a little dance, on and off the kerb. His belly jiggles. Toby puts his thumbs into the belt-loops on his jeans and grins. I turn round and walk away from them towards the shop. I'm glad I was with Ralph instead of them last night.

'Awwwwwww, Mikey-Mikey, don't be like that!' Jim runs and walks on one side of me. He flings his arm round my shoulder. I make my fingers go stiff. He squeezes me. I stop. I groan. Jim takes a step away from me, hands held high.

'Hey, just joking around!' He rolls his eyes to Toby. 'No bloody sense of humour today!'

Toby shakes his head and tuts at me with sparkly eyes. I don't like it when it's just Toby and Jim.

'Where's Dave?'

The lads look at each other. They stop smiling.

'He's not well,' says Jim.

'Had an accident,' says Toby.

I stop walking and turn to look at them. They're not messing around. There's a funny whooshing noise in my ears. I lean against the wall.

'When?'

Jim clears his throat. 'Last night . . . he . . . The doctor says he'll be up on his feet again soon.'

'I like Dave.'

'I like Dave.' Toby copies me in a baby-voice and pulls a face. Jim ignores him. Toby goes a bit red.

'He's a good lad.' Jim nods.

'What happened to him?' I *do* like Dave. Happy face. Wonky smile. I screw up my nose. How can I help? 'Ralph was looking for him last night. He's my mate.' The lads jump when I say that. I puff my chest out. See, lads? I have a mate too! 'Maybe he'll look out for Dave if I ask him.'

The lads look at each other. Big Rick's lorry goes past. He honks his horn when he sees me and waves as he goes by. I wave too. Toby coughs.

'Dave'll tell you what happened when he's out.' Jim sucks through his teeth, eyes thin.

He's got a funny look on his face. I don't know what it means. He punches my arm and walks off.

'Seeeeeeee yooooouuuuuu, Mikey!' He pulls a moony at me.

Toby snorts and runs after him.

'Yeah, seeeeeeeee yoooooooooooouuuuuuuu!'

Timmer growls and follows me as I walk off to the shop. I drag my heels.

I spend ages choosing the cakes in the shop. It's my favourite bit of shopping. The shop-man hasn't got any cakes with cherries on the top like it says on Pat's list so that means I can pick them: the shop-man said so. I get a doughnut with white icing and rainbow sprinkles, a chocolate muffin, a flapjack and a rum ball. The chocolate muffin is mine for scoffing on the way home though. If I knew where Dave lives, I could take him one too.

The pavement is cracked so I make sure my feet tap in each bit between the cracks as I go. The cake is good—makes me feel better. Timmer is getting fed up because it makes me slow and because I haven't given him anything to eat. I'll give you some dog-biscuits when we get home Timmer.

I stay away from the bus-shelter on my way back. Even from the other side of the street, I can see the glass is covered with ice that cracks and shifts to make me look at it. I sneak a quick peek—**the two men are still there, tramp-shape and Dad-shape** . . . I walk away fast, fast, fast. I don't want to see.

My head is starting to hurt. The tramp is dead. Dave is ill. Mum is ill. I don't know where Dad is but he's not in prison. I walk even faster. The lads are up ahead. I turn into the alley because I don't want to see them again.

Timmer looks up, trotting next to me. He doesn't like it when I'm like this. I slow down and sit by the gutter, pull Timmer to me. He whines and rests his head on my knee. I take a deep breath in and it's so cold that my nose burns. I breathe out dragon-smoke.

Winter breath on a summer day.

I go still. I can feel someone staring at me. I don't want to look up. This bit of alley comes out near the old-garage land. We've come here by accident. I take a peek sideways.

There's a man, all hunched over, standing at the end of the alley. Staring at me.

I stare back. My heart is going fast fast fast.

It's the tramp.

Behind him, the shadows on the old-garage land are waking up. The Backwards in the garage hasn't finished yet.

The tramp shuffles away, a little way up the road with his back to me. Big floppy hat. Black long coat.

It's funny, but I never really saw him walking before. He was always sitting down somewhere. I'm not going to follow him, Timmer. I only want to see nice Backwards, like Dad and Little Mikey by the river or the cow being born.

The tramp keeps going but he's slow. He's got this upsy-downsy walk. Something is wrong with his right foot.

I sit up straight.

Someone else had an upsy-downsy walk. Who was it, Timmer, who was it? We saw him the other day . . . My hands go sweaty. Timmer looks up at me and whines.

It was the nasty-Bill-garage man. We saw him by the river.

I drop the shopping bag. The carrots roll onto the pavement. I feel dizzy. The same walk. The same squidgy big nose. Both with curly black hair. My chest is going tight tight tight. Did the tramp used to be the nasty-Bill-garage man? Is it the same person?

Shadows dance with boots on in my head. Clompy boots. I see the tramp wriggling out of the broken deckchair. Dad's scared face in the woods looking for Bill. Dad's big clompy boots kicking kicking kicking . . .

I wrap my arms around me tight, tight, tight.

Dad. Dad.

It *was* you, after all, wasn't it? You were getting Bill back for leaving you in the woods, weren't you?

Chapter Twenty-Two

The garage-man-tramp worked with Dad and Ralph. They all knew each other. Frost snaps in my nostrils and in my belly. I didn't know. I didn't know. I didn't know. But I'm working it out, bit by bit. I *am*.

The tramp is nearly at the bend in the road now, walking his upsy-downsy walk.

I follow with Timmer. I clench my fists. He cheated on Dad—let the police catch him and Dad was only doing the burning for me and Mum. My legs start to run all by themselves.

All their faces are mashing together in my head like scrambled eggs—tramp—Dad—Ralph—garage man. The world is topsy-whirly and I hold on to Timmer because he's the only thing that feels really Now.

The tramp is slowing down. We are near the burned-out

garage. This is where he's going. He stands and stares. This is where he used to be the garage man, Bill. He stinks of pee and firewater. His face is dirty. Spit is dribbling into his beard.

I lean right up to him so I nearly touch his squishy purple nose and jab my finger at him.

'You promised Dad you'd look out for him.' My voice is like Timmer's snarl. 'You promised you'd see him right. But you didn't. You let the black-and-whites get him.'

The tramp can't hear me. I reach for his shoulder but my arm just passes straight through.

He lifts his dirty hand and wipes his dirty face. He sniffs. He's crying. He's watching the burned-out garage land and he's crying. Could you see the Backwards too, tramp? Could you see it as well?

He sniffs again. He pulls out a bottle from inside his dirty black coat. He starts to drink. Not little bits. Big gulps like he's really thirsty. His eyes go wobbly. He burps and spins round to the street. A lady is walking by with a red pushchair.

'The Fiiiiiiire!' he hisses at her. His eyes are bloodshot.

The lady jerks her head up. She puts her hand in front of her sleeping baby's face like she doesn't want him to see it.

The tramp leans towards her, wobbling as he points back at the empty garage land. 'The Flaaaaaamessssssssssssssss!'

The lady won't look at him. She pushes her pushchair away from him and walks faster.

'Shhhhhhhhhhhhhhhhhh!' He lifts his dirty finger to his lips as she walks past. 'Shhhhhhhhhhhhhhh!' He leans after her as if he's telling her a secret but his voice is loud. 'Don't tell . . . mustn't tell.' He shakes his head.

I sit on the rubble pile at the edge of where the garage used to be. The Backwards swirls are pulling me further back.

The tramp is still bending forwards, but he's disappearing too.

The burned garage shape on the ground is a great open mouth and it's trying to suck me in.

I put my arms around Timmer's neck and hold my fingers tight. I want to see what happened in here. I want to bloody see what Bill did to my dad.

It's night-time. Ralph and the garage-man-tramp are sitting in the garage by a little table, drinking a beer. There are papers all over the table. Papers with numbers on them. There's a radio playing some music. Where's Dad? I spin round in a circle. It makes me dizzy but I see him. Well, I see a bit of him. His legs are sticking out from under a white Morris minor. I recognize his orange and purple stripy socks. I bought him them for Christmas one year. I chose them myself. He is humming to the song on the radio. He likes singing.

'How you doing there, Stu?' says the garage-man-tramp.

Dad pushes himself out on the car-creeper and sits up.

243

His face is dirty. He's holding a spanner and he drops it. The clang makes my teeth ache.

'Nearly there, Bill, just a little while more. Half an hour or so.'

'Every bit of overtime helps, hey, mate?'

Dad nods and yawns. Under the dirt, he's tired.

Ralph is shuffling a pack of cards. The cards are blue and dog-eared. He's got this funny grin on his face. The light hanging from the ceiling isn't very strong. Perfect for shadows.

'You know, I've thought of an idea so that Stu can earn a bit more money.'

The garage-man-tramp gives a big sigh, closes his eyes and rubs the side of his head near his eyes in circles. 'I know, Ralph, but I haven't decided that yet . . . '

Ralph keeps shuffling and smiling. He leans over to switch the radio off.

'Leave it!' The garage-man-tramp holds up his hand. 'Stu and I need our music, don't we?'

Dad smiles and makes crinkles at the edge of his eyes. 'You've got more work needs doing?' He leans his head back against the side of the Morris minor.

'Nah.' The garage-man-tramp picks up a handful of the papers and drops them, one by one, back on the table. 'Bills, bills, bills . . . That, my man, is the problem.'

'But I have offered a solution,' says Ralph. 'A practical solution. That's what you pay your premiums for.'

'What premiums?' asks Dad.

'Insurance premiums, mate.' Ralph cuts the pack then mixes them by flicking them together with his thumbs. 'Insured risk—fire damage.'

'What, burn the place down and claim the insurance money?' asks Dad.

The garage-man-tramp groans and puts his head in his hands.

Ralph grins and starts shuffling his cards again. 'You said it, mate, not me.'

Dad stands up, his mouth is a bit open, and goes to join them at the table. He picks up a beer and flicks the top off on the side of the table.

'That's illegal, ain't it?'

'Loads of people do it. It's all factored into the premium,' says Ralph. I can see his knee has started jiggling under the table. I stand behind Dad. I want to lean against him.

'Factored into the premium, you say?' says Dad.

The garage-man-tramp groans again, shaking his head.

'Don't know what your problem is, Bill. You were always a risk-taker, a man that made things happen. You'd get a packet for this place. Buy yourself a place in the sun. Just a little cut for Stu for striking the match. A little cut for me for my organizational skills and experience.' He winks at Dad. 'I got it all sussed out, me. Can't go wrong.'

'What? Me strike a match?' Dad says, quick as anything.

The garage-man-tramp takes his head out of his hands.

His eyes are all wrinkly at the edges. His hands shake as they rest on the table.

'You worked hard for this place, mate,' says Ralph. 'This little bill problem you have,' he flicks his thumb at the papers on the table, 'means you might lose it anyway. Why not be smart and get ahead of the game and make yourself a nest egg?'

The garage-man-tramp's mouth is set in a hard line. He frowns but still doesn't say anything.

'Stu and me—we'll help you out, won't we, mate?' Ralph smiles at Dad.

Dad takes a long swig of beer.

'I'm not sure if this is right, you know . . . '

'Bill'd make it worth your while, wouldn't you, Bill? Could take Lisa and the little 'un on holiday. Somewhere glitzy. Your missus, she needs a break, you said so yourself.'

Dad nods. He frowns and looks from Ralph to the garage-man-tramp and back again. The garage-man-tramp smiles a slow sad smile and runs his fingers along the pile of bills.

The wind blows and the light bulb dangling from the ceiling goes to and fro. It makes dark shapes dance on the wall.

Dad runs his hands through his hair. The garage-man-tramp looks at him for a long time and then raises his eyebrows.

Dad clears his throat.

216

Chapter Twenty-Two

'What sort of sums are we talking about here, then?' he says.

Ralph's face nearly splits in two with a huge huge smile. The garage-man-tramp gives a long sigh and picks up a pencil and a calculator.

Chapter Twenty-Three

The Backwards fades. It's just me and Timmer and the burned garage land.

Ralph was in it too. Ralph wanted them to do the burning. He wants me to do the burning. Me and Dad. Like father, like son, he said. Dad wanted to get some money so we could go on holiday. To the beach?

All these people knew each other. They all knew Dad. My whirly dream is in my head again—fire and smoke and Dad and Ralph and the tramp all spinning and spinning and spinning.

Got to get my head straight, Timmer. I've got to go to the river.

I start to run—past the old library, round the corner, over the scrubland-before-the-fields, over the fence, into the field, arms out and run run run. Timmer barks and chases smells across the grass. The wind pushes in my face and I open my mouth wide so it can go inside and blow all the shadows and smoke and fire and rubbish away high into the sky, far far away over the farm, over the fields and the cows and the trees—all the way to the sea.

My eyes sting. *I'm* not going to the sea like Mum promised. Nothing nice happens to *me*. Only bad nasty muddly stuff.

My head twizzles again. Ralph knew about Dad's burning. Ralph knew the tramp-garage-man. I don't know why it's all wrong but it is. I groan and crouch down so I'm as small as I can be. I hold my arms over my head and close my eyes. Timmer pushes against my legs and scratches at me.

I look up and see the farm, just up the hill a little way. The cows are being taken back to the fields after milking. I wonder if Meg's there today. She told me to be careful about Ralph. Maybe she was right. I want to talk to Cackler. When I'm with them, the Backwards is good and everything is all right. Things get better. I start to run again.

The farmyard is empty. There's a stack of green plastic barrels near the gates, all neat and tidy. The Land Rover isn't here. The farmhouse door is shut, the curtains closed. I stand at the gate. I don't know what to do now. Timmer sniffs behind the barrels.

'Hey, Mikey!' Ralph steps out of his shed. He's wiping his hands on a rag. His face is sweaty. 'Just trying to mend an old tractor engine while I'm off milking duties.' He smiles. 'How's my mate?'

I don't smile. Timmer growls. My head is sludging up. I don't know what to do.

'Everything all right, Mikey? Got a bit of a hangover after last night?'

I nod to the last bit. My head still hurts. 'You knew the tramp was the garage man. You knew them both. And Dad!' I shout it out. I didn't mean to but it comes out loud.

Ralph's eyebrows go up. 'But you already know that, Mikey. I showed you the photo, remember? Me and your dad and Bill. We all worked in the garage together.' He smiles but he's shading his eyes from the sun so I can't see them. 'What's the problem with that? We're all mates together.'

All my head is going black. What *is* the problem with that? I make my fingers go stiff. Ralph told me all about it when I was at his house. Ralph didn't do anything wrong, did he? My head hurts. My head hurts. The Backwards is making me all tangly and muddly.

'I've nearly finished here for the day. Why don't you come back for a cup of tea, hey? Back to my place?'

'Is Meg here?'

Ralph raises his eyebrows. 'Ahhhhh, so that's the reason for your visit! Little horn-dog! Nope, out with her gramps.'

My face burns. Now he's here, it all seems wrong. He's

being my mate, just like normal. Isn't he? I want to talk to Meg. I want to talk to Mum. I don't know what to do.

'She'll be back tomorrow though. I'll tell her you paid her a surprise visit.' He winks. He's enjoying this. 'C'mon. I've had a long day. I need a cup of tea with my mate Mikey.'

'See, I'm a bit worried about Dave.'

'Why's that, Mikey?'

We're drinking tea outside Ralph's house, sitting on the ground and leaning against the wall. The sun is going down behind the trees. It's nearly gone. The sky is bleeding red and orange into the sky. It looks like that watercolour paint stuff at school, when you wet the paper and then let the colours spread. I like doing it because the paint goes on further than you think it would, like it's got a life of its own.

Ralph waves his hands across my eyes.

'Hey, why are you worried about Dave, dreamer-boy? He's a lazy good-for-nothing. Not helpful like you, Mikey.'

I smile. 'He's ill. His mates said so.'

'You spoke to his mates today?'

I nod. The stars are coming out too. There aren't any clouds so I will be able to see loads of them.

'What'd they say, Mikey?'

I look up at the stars. They aren't very clear yet

though—I'll have to wait till it gets darker to see them properly.

'Hey?' I just notice that Ralph is staring hard at me. 'Nothing, nothing much. He's ill. And I said maybe you could look out for him cos you're a good mate.'

Ralph's mouth twitches at the edges. 'And what did they say to that?'

'They said Dave would talk to me when he's better.'

'I bet they bloody did.'

Ralph slaps me on the back. I sigh and lean into the bricks but the house shadows suck at my scar so I sit back up straight.

'And you're going to help with my little job aren't you, Mikey?' He winks at me.

'The burning?'

He nods.

My belly goes cold. The sun has gone now. It's nearly night. The evening wind is warm against my face. It makes me shiver.

'Tomorrow night's the night, mate. OK with you?'

I chew on my lip. Timmer looks up at me. He whines and paws at my leg. I stroke his fur but I still don't feel warm. I don't know about the burning now. Dad did it and it went wrong. It made lots of problems.

'You got plans tomorrow night, Mikey?'

'No.'

'That's set then. Good man.' Ralph raises his mug and

clinks it against mine. 'It's the house with the boarded-up windows right at the end of your street—past the library, past the old garage that your dad and I used to work at—all the way to the end. You know it?'

'The one where the gypsies used to live?'

Ralph smiles. 'Yep. I've got rid of them gypsies though.'

'Whose house is it?'

His smile gets wider. 'Mine, mate. Inherited it but it needs doing up and I don't have the cash.' He pats me on the arm. 'Just a paperwork thing, mate, that's all. No harm to anyone.'

Ralph stretches out, like a cat in the sun. 'I'll put the petrol in that blue can there and leave it for you with matches in the kitchen. Easy peasy. Just make sure you splash it around properly before you strike a match and then get out quick. The back door will be unlocked. Then meet me back here, OK?'

I'm not sure I want to do this any more. I don't know what to say though. I've never had a proper mate since I was Little Mikey—except Timmer. I don't want to be a bad 'un to Ralph. But I don't want to be a bad 'un and do a burning and go to prison.

'No one will get hurt?'

'No one, mate. I'll check beforehand, then I'll call your home three times on the phone. Three rings. Don't answer. OK? Then you come back here and I'll have sorted it all. Can't go wrong.'

Timmer stands up and walks away from me, up the garden path and sits by the gate. He looks up at the sky. The moonlight shines on his back and head. What shall I do, Timmer?

'Where will you be?'

'Pub with friends but I'll be back here to meet you. Promise, Mikey. Then we'll plan a trip out to celebrate. What do you reckon? You wanted a trip to the beach, didn't you? You choose, mate, you choose and we'll do it.'

The beach? I'd *love* that!! The sea goes on and on— it's even better than the river. Sort of. Timmer knows I'm happy and trots back to me.

'The beach'd be great! Could we go, Ralph?'

Ralph looks serious and holds out his hand. 'Shake on it then, Mikey. Deal?'

'Deal!'

All the world is silent. All the trees are listening. What are you doing, Mikey? What are you doing? The wind blows around my head. I've shaken hands but I was thinking about the beach, not the burning. I don't want to think about the burning.

I look at the Mini in the garden. Dad could mend it. Dad wouldn't leave it broken down there for ages.

'Have you found anything out about Dad, Ralph?'

Ralph gulps his tea and then burps.

'Well, I got as far as you did. You're right. He isn't in prison any more.' He watches me out the corner of his eye.

'You know it might be best just to leave it. Let it go.'

I rub Timmer's ears and he pushes close to my leg. I shake my head. My chest aches. 'No, I can't do that.'

Ralph puts down his mug. He looks me straight in the face. 'What difference does it make, mate? Really? He hasn't been here for ages. He's not here now either, wherever he is. It doesn't matter does it? It's all the same to you.'

I clutch hard on to Timmer. It does matter to me, it does matter to me, it does it does itdoesitdoesitdoesit-doesitdoesitdoes. He's my dad. My head is starting to stretch because all the shadows in there are getting angry. They are stomping so hard my scar will rip open. My dad. My dad.

'It does matter where he is.' My voice wobbles. 'It does.'

'But WHY? I know he's your dad but you've managed without him, really well, you and your mum, haven't you?'

My voice is little and gulpy. 'You said you'd find him if I got Dave for you.'

Ralph puts his hand on my back. 'Mate, I've done my best. I swear on my life.'

My scar aches. The shadows are going mad. The boots are kicking the tramp. Those clompy big boots.

'But what about the tramp?' My voice has nearly gone.

'What?' Ralph's hand pushes against me. 'What about the tramp?'

'I saw Dad's work-boots kicking him. I'm worried that he . . . I'm scared it was . . . '

The shadows fly into the night sky, screeching to the stars.

Ralph takes his hand from my back. His face is close to mine. His breath smells scary and his eyes are red. He breathes big breaths in and out of his nose. I'm frightened. I move away from him.

'You saw the tramp being killed?'

My head is pressing against the bricks. I try to move away more but Ralph's face is too close. Timmer growls.

'A bit of it,' I whisper.

Ralph grabs my face and looks into my eyes like he's trying to get in my head. Then he lets me go.

He sits back, chewing his lip. Above us, my shadows are still going mental against the stars. They scream and scream and scream and I can't make them stop.

I want to go home. I don't like it here any more.

'I'm off now, Ralph.' I start to walk down the path and whistle for Timmer to follow me.

Ralph gets up and grabs my arm. 'See you tomorrow night—you won't forget now will you, Mikey?'

I pull away but he holds it tighter.

His mouth stretches into a smile. 'Don't leave in a huff. I know it was sad about the tramp, but we're friends now, aren't we?' He squeezes my arm. 'Aren't we?'

I nod but I keep looking at the ground. 'It's time for me to go now.'

Ralph sucks through his teeth. His eyes go thin.

'But thanks for the tea.'

'Till tomorrow?'

'OK.'

I walk with Timmer to the gate and turn into the woods. Once Ralph can't see me any more, I run as fast as I can and don't stop until I get home.

Chapter Twenty-Four

I can hear the shed-shadows all night long. Something terrible is happening. Something terrible has happened. They sing it to me. They stamp and scream and shout. I put my head under the pillows but they are even louder in my head. They come into my room, under my bed, and whisper black secrets to me.

As soon as it gets light, I'm out of here. I sit up in bed, push my back next to the wall and pull the duvet under my nose.

I wait for the sun.

The grey light comes first. It's sort of like a ghost of the real sun. The black in my room goes a bit. I stand by the back window, still all wrapped up as snug as a bug in a rug. Our garden is the darkest. The shed is the blackest of all. I breathe on the window and the world swirls behind the mist.

In the scrubland-before-the-fields, Little Mikey kicks a football to Little Dave, whizzing across the grass. I swallow hard. My scar made me forget about that. Dave and me played together when we were small.

Little Dave kicks the ball towards our fence and it thuds, smack!

'Goooooooooal' yells Little Dave, arms up, running with his little legs. Little Mikey jumps on his back, whooping.

I rub my eyes and they've gone. Where is Dave now? What happened to him?

Behind the scrubland, there's the field that goes over a little hill and back down to the river. I can't see the river but I can feel her. I can always feel her. Then behind that, there's the wood and the hill behind Cackler's farm. That's where the sun is coming. There's a mist and I can only see the shape of the trees. I hug my arms round me tight.

The sun is peeping out from behind the trees on the hill. The sky is pink and orange and yellow—it's starting to burn. Fingers of light are going down the hill. The cows will feel them first.

That's good. Old Mary and her calf, and Bess and her little one and all the others will be there. They'll be getting ready to be milked. They'll be standing by the gate, waiting for Cackler or Ralph to fetch them. I smile.

Ralph said Meg would be back today. I pull on my

jeans and trainers and T-shirt. I can't stay in here any more, Timmer. Not today.

Pat hears me as I go downstairs. 'Hey, Mikey, you off already? I never see you, you're so busy!'

I stop halfway down. Please let me go. 'I need the river.'

She puts her head over the banisters. Her face has red lines down it from where she's been lying on her pillow and her hair's squashed flat on one side. 'I spoke to your mum last night.' She smiles. 'You might get a nice surprise soon.'

I jump. The burning? Does Pat know about the burning?

'I think, *think*, she'll be coming home, maybe today maybe tomorrow.' Pat's smile gets bigger. 'How's that for a good surprise?'

'MUM! TONIGHT?' I do my bendy-leg dance and nearly fall down the stairs, grab the banister quick. Timmer barks.

'Steady on, Mikey!' Pat is laughing. 'So you're not disappointed, let's just think it'll be tomorrow. Any earlier will be a bonus then, won't it?'

'Tomorrow,' I sing to Timmer. He howls back. 'Tomorrow, tomorrow . . .'

I stop by the river first to see if I can see my bittern. I don't walk all the way up to my fishing spot. I just stay near the path to Cackler's farm. Where are you, bittern? Where are you?

Timmer sits quiet. I hold his nose so he can't make a noise.

Shhhhhhhhhhh. She'll never come out if you make a fuss, doggy-dog. He snorts into my hand. He wants to be running around.

Hey, look! There's something moving in the rushes. I squat down and lean forwards. A baby duck swims out into the river. There's another—and another! And here's the mum. I rest on my heels and rock onto my toes and back. All fluffy and new.

I reach down into the river and hold my hand there. It's cold and sparkly. I flick my hand up and splash Timmer. He jumps away, barking. I drop back so I'm lying on the grass, looking up at the sky. I close my eyes. I'm tired. The sun is hot. It's quiet. The river keeps on going and going.

Stand guard, Timmer. Look after me. I'm just going to rest for a bit.

'Mikey!'

Where am I? In a dream? In bed?

'Mikey! Your face is all red!'

I sit up. I can't see for a minute. The world is all stars. My face is hot. I shiver inside and close my eyes for a minute. Burning. Flames. Fire. That's what I'm doing tonight. The burning. My head is red red red. It makes my legs jiggle to think of it.

'Are you all right, Mikey?'

There's a soft hand on my shoulder. I open one eye. Meg's sitting cross-legged, watching me. She smells of flowers today.

'You're really sunburned, Mikey. How long have you been here? Ralph said you came to look for me yesterday.'

'I couldn't sleep last night. Came here when the sun got up.' My arms are hot too.

Meg pulls some thick grasses from the riverbank and starts to wind them together to make a plait.

'Why couldn't you sleep?'

'I'm helping Ralph tonight and I was worried because . . . '

I stop.

Meg looks up at me.

I moan and put my hands on my head. I bet I wasn't supposed to say anything. The words just came out. I twist my fingers together. I look out to the wood and then at Meg and she's still looking at me so I look the other way to the bridge and then back at Meg but she hasn't moved. I moan again.

'How are you helping him?' Meg's voice is quiet.

'It's just a little thing . . . '

Her eyebrows go up.

'No one gets hurt, Ralph said so.'

232

'*Hurt?*' Meg drops her grass plait. 'What are you doing for him, Mikey?'

'It's . . . ' What did Ralph say? What did he say? I screw up my face. He said it was . . . 'a paperwork thing and then I meet him back at his place later tonight.'

'A *paperwork* thing?'

I nod but I don't look at her green green eyes. Timmer wanders over and puts his head on Meg's knee. MEG's knee, Timmer? You're my dog, not hers! She strokes his ears and he licks her knee. I kick at a stone. Hard.

'Gramps has always told me not to speak badly of Ralph—give him a second chance. But I'm worried, Mikey.' Meg is frowning. 'Ralph is tricking you; he's not a paperwork person.'

I clench my teeth. 'He's my mate.'

'He doesn't have mates, Mikey. He just looks after Number One.'

She's talking too quick after everything I say. I feel the jabs in my head and put my fingers next to my eyes, in the little dip-bit, and press hard like Mum does sometimes.

'Number One?'

'He just looks after himself, Mikey.' Meg shakes her head at me. 'I *told* you before, be careful.' Her voice is getting louder.

I clench my fists together. There's something building up in my chest. It's getting bigger and bigger and it's starting to hurt. Ralph is my *mate*. Meg is my *mate*. Ralph is going to give me some pocket money and we're going to the beach after the burning. That's what he said, didn't he? DIDN'T HE?

'You listening, Mikey? He's not always nice. I've seen him sometimes at the farm with the animals.'

I bite my lip. I've seen him too, sometimes, but he said he was just playing around. Like with Timmer. He didn't actually *hurt* them, did he? DID he?

Meg puts her hands on my arms and her face is really close to mine.

'This is important! Be careful, Mikey!'

I put my hands over my ears and I start to rock to and fro, to and fro. I can't work it out. I don't know why it's all wrong but it is. All these people know each other and I didn't know and Dad's escaped from prison and maybe he killed the tramp and the Backwards is always waiting for me and Mum's gone all weird and sad and I DON'T UNDERSTAND! Timmer whines and sits closer to me.

'Stop it, Meg!' To and fro, to and fro. 'You're waking up the shadows! You're making my head hurt!'

Meg lets go straight away.

''S OK, Mikey, 's OK. Please stop . . . ' Her voice goes all gentle.

'I wanted to go to the beach like I used to when I was Little Mikey and Ralph's going to take me . . . '

''S OK, Mikey. 'S OK . . . '

To and fro, to and fro.

'I wouldn't hurt anyone . . . Never!'

To and fro, to and fro.

'Of *course* you wouldn't!'

'Promise me you won't tell anyone about this paper-work thing!'

Meg flinches as she watches me.

I pull my hair HARD. 'PROMISE!'

'OK, Mikey. OK.' Her voice is so quiet I can hardly hear it. It makes me quiet too.

I stop rocking. I shiver. I watch her. Meg moves back and sits down, crosses her legs.

'Of course you wouldn't hurt anyone, Mikey.' She smiles and her freckles dance. 'I just want you to be all right, that's all. You're my friend too, you know.'

'Really?'

'Of course!'

The light is sparkly on the river. Timmer wags his tail. We watch the wind blow the reeds and the leaves on the trees. I love the shushing sound it makes.

Meg looks at me. 'Can I ask you a question, Mikey?'

'Huh?'

She picks at the edge of her sleeve. 'What did you mean, just now, about waking up the shadows?'

The shadows? My chest goes tight. I pick up the grass plait that Meg made and twist it round my fingers. 'You'll think I'm a nutter.'

'No I won't.' She goes quiet. 'But it's OK if you don't want to talk about it.'

I watch the wind blow her hair around. Her eyes are kind. I think I do want to—I *do* want to tell Meg. I take a deep breath. 'The shadows wake up when I worry. Like they're alive.'

I look at her to see if she's laughing at me, but she isn't. Her face is soft. She nods.

'But they're changing. Getting bigger. Louder.' I screw up my face. This isn't coming out right. 'Getting right inside my head and outside it too . . .' I stop talking. I'm just so STUPID with words.

'When do they grow like that?' She watches me as she pulls a thread on her sleeve.

'I dunno. When something's wrong.' I frown. What about the ones in Little Mikey's room? *They* didn't get bigger. 'They go quiet when I've seen . . . seen . . . their stuff.' I look up. That sounds rubbish.

Meg chews her lip. 'That sort of makes sense. Kind of looking them in the face?'

I shrug. I've not been *that* brave with the shadows but I don't want to tell Meg that. Talking about them makes me want to close down. I just want them to go away. I hug my legs close and put my chin on my knees. Timmer gives a big sigh. 'I don't want to talk about it any more.'

'OK.' Meg smiles, then starts to giggle. She points at my arms. 'Your skin is really red . . .'

She's right. It is. I walk down to the river and hold my arms under the water. The river makes them nice and cold. I can see myself in the water looking back up at me. Blond hair. Blue eyes. Red cheeks. I close my eyes and stick my head under water. Bubbles come out of my nose. The river is everywhere. Cold. Quiet. Safe.

I come back up again to the noise of the wind and the tractor far away. My eyes are pulled to the other riverbank, to the reeds. For a minute, I don't see anything but the swishing reeds. Then I spot her.

Oh, *she's* here!

I sit down quietly and hold Timmer's nose so he can't bark. I wave at Meg to come over too. Quiet, Meg, quiet. She comes over without a noise and sits beside me.

What? her green eyes say. *What is it, Mikey?*

I nod to the reeds.

My bittern stands still. Her neck is stretched with the beak to the sky.

Meg's eyes go bigger. She looks at me. She's surprised.

I hold my breath and press Timmer down to the grass. The wind ruffles the reeds. The stripes on her neck feathers are like the lines of the reeds. A disguise. The wind blows and she moves side to side, so that the stripes and the reeds move together. Her yellow eyes aren't looking up though. They are staring straight at us.

A tingle rushes down my arms. Meg looks at me. I look at Meg. Just look at that! Just look! Meg smiles.

Then she's off. My bittern steps back into the reeds. The wind blows again. She's gone. Gone.

Meg breathes out slowly. 'Would you believe it? Would you believe it . . . ' She shakes her head so all the curls bob up and down.

I smile. I'm glad Meg was here. No one else has seen her. Just me and Meg. I squeeze her shoulder. 'This is our little secret.'

Meg smiles back as she stands up.

'It is, Mikey. It is. This secret is safe with me.' She picks up her bag and yawns. 'I've got to go back to the farm now. Afternoon jobs with Gramps. We're moving the cows down to this field by the river—they've made a right mess of the one they're in.' She rolls her eyes and walks back to the path. 'But Mikey?'

I turn round. 'What?'

'If you want to chat about anything else—you know, any other secrets that worry you and mean you can't sleep . . . I can keep those secrets too, you know.'

She pulls the bag onto her shoulder and starts to walk back to the farm. The sun makes her hair look nearly yellow, not brown.

'Thanks, Meg,' I call out but my voice is quiet and I don't think she can hear me.

Chapter Twenty-Five

Three rings. This is it. This is the time for the burning.

Pat's on lates again. It's just me and Timmer. It's always just me and Timmer.

Timmer is drinking water out of his bowl. He's so noisy when he drinks but he doesn't sit down like normal when he's finished. He knows something is up.

My hands are shaking. My stomach is all fizzy. It's dark outside but it's dark in my head too. I hop from one foot to the other. I can't wait and watch TV any more, Timmer-dog. It's time to go. Time to help Ralph with the burning. Shall we do it? Shall we?

I put my chips in the bin. I can't eat tonight.

Everything is still. Everything is dark. I can hear my heart thud thud thudding. All the trees outside, all the shadows, everything is leaning in, watching what I'm going to do.

I go to the back door and pass the kitchen mirror. Out the corner of my eye, I see Dad staring out of it at me. His face is all dirty from smoke and he looks worried. Just for a flash. I stop. It was from when *he* did his burning too. I go back. I hold my breath. I take a look.

Nothing.

He's gone. It's just me.

Me, Mikey, before I do the burning.

Mum has left the brown envelope poking out of the side of the fridge where she tried to hide it. I pull it out. There's a photo sticking out. Me and Dad and Mum on the beach. All of us, smiling. I touch the picture and it feels warm. I can smell the sea. I put it in my jeans pocket. I want Mum and Dad with me today as well as Timmer. Then I put the brown envelope back next to the fridge just like it was before. Timmer goes out the door first and I go after him as it clicks shut behind me.

All the way up the street, it's as quiet as quiet as quiet. Everyone is inside. Some people leave their curtains open so I can see them. Gavin'n'Tina have shut theirs but I can see Albert watching TV with his big brown slippers up on the coffee table. The man with the hairy back is walking up and down his lounge shouting down the phone. His face is all red and puffy. At Jim's house, they are all eating fish and chips out of newspaper on their knees.

I keep walking. Timmer stays close.

The burning. The burning. The burning.

What's going to happen, Timmer? What's going to happen? I can't see my house any more. Shall I go back? Wait for Pat to come home? But Ralph is waiting for *me*. I start walking to the burning place again. It gets darker.

And colder.

There's a light on at the bus-shelter as I walk past. A little room in the dark. They're there again, the two of them, the tramp shouting at the Dad-shape . . .

I walk past quick quick quick. STILL there? The Backwards keeps on playing in there. Over and over again. The two men arguing and arguing and arguing . . . I clench my teeth.

I DON'T LIKE THIS! I didn't ask for this! I don't want to have to see Dad's Backwards. I start to run. The shadows clap to make me go faster . . . Timmer barks and jumps at me.

Stop it, mutt! Just stop it!!! You're slowing me down!

Why is the Backwards doing this?

Why won't it all stop?

WHY WON'T IT LEAVE ME ALONE?

I slow down at the phone box, lean my hands against the glass and take in big big breaths.

Deep down, I know the answer. It's because the Backwards story hasn't finished yet. That's why it's still here, pulling at me. It's because Dad's burning wasn't the right thing, was it?

I don't want to look at the nasty Backwards. I don't want to see Dad kill the tramp. I don't want to see bad things.

Timmer licks my hand and sits on my foot. He looks up at me. He hates it when I'm upset. He whines and pushes his nose in my hand.

If I let all this start, Timmer-dog, it'll wash all over me and carry me on until it's over, I know it will. I'll have to see it all.

I sit on the pavement. I squash an old can with my foot. Ralph will be waiting for me. He gave me the three rings. But I have to check the Backwards, don't I? Before I do the burning, in case it all goes wrong . . . Am I brave enough, Timmer? Will it make it better if I do it? For me, for Dave, for Mum . . . for Dad?

I walk slowly back to the bus-shelter. I scuff my heels in the earth. Timmer stays close. He leans into me, warm and safe. I stop to stroke his head. It won't get any easier if I go slow, though. I pull my hand away and keep walking.

Best get it over with. The world swirls. Frost crackles up the bus-shelter glass.

Two people are standing on the pavement just up from me. I know them.

I walk over—they can't see me but I can see them. I lean against the street-light to listen.

The tramp steps forward. He straightens his collar so he

looks a little bit like the garage man. This is strange—him being one person and then another. But if I look carefully, I can tell he's the same underneath. It's his eyes. They haven't changed except they look more sad when he's the tramp.

The Dad-shaped man turns to face the tramp.

My stomach goes tight. I don't want to see Dad here in this Backwards.

'What's your problem, Ralph Jackson?' says the tramp.

Ralph? Ralph not Dad? The frost creeps down my throat, in my ears, down my eyes . . . RALPH?

Ralph looks different too. He needs to shave and his face is sneery. When he smiles it doesn't reach his eyes.

'My problem is that Stuart ballsed up. He got caught. He made a mess of things as usual.' Ralph rolls his eyes.

My stomach goes all tense. That isn't right. Dad doesn't mess things up. I saw him in the woods. Someone called the police. He was set up. Dad is good at things. He can mend cars and make Mum's eyes shine. The shadows whistle around me but I tell them to bloody shut up. Shut up! I have to concentrate. This is my dad he's talking about.

'The jury's out on that one, Ralph Jackson.' The tramp's eyes go squinty. 'There was a tip-off and we both know it. The police were in the woods before I arrived. Now who would have told them that, I wonder?' He breathes hard down his nose.

I lean in because his voice is really low. You can smell angry things on his breath.

Ralph leans forward towards the tramp. 'What are you saying, William?'

'You never liked Stuart, we both know that too.'

My stomach lurches. I can't see properly because my eyes have gone all watery. What is the tramp saying? He and Dad were together on the photo. They were mates too. All mates together, that's what Ralph said.

Ralph sucks air through his teeth and smiles the hardest smile I have ever seen.

I put my hands over my ears but then I take them away again because it doesn't make any difference. I can still hear the Backwards even if I shut my ears.

'Not relevant, William. But I will tell you the facts that are relevant. One: you are involved in an insurance scam. Two: I was not involved—I didn't torch the place, I didn't sign any statements to an insurance company. Three: you go to prison for fraud if anyone hears about this.' Ralph's smile isn't a smile at all any more.

The tramp pulls back. His eyes are so thin that they are just little black lines.

'Now, William, you know what Fact Number Four is, don't you?'

'You bastard.' The tramp spits it out.

Ralph leans closer. 'No, William—you fool. I set the whole thing up and you still screwed it up. What happened? No

garage. No livelihood. Rejected claim. No money.' He pulls his lips back so his teeth show. He doesn't look like Ralph at all. 'Leave Stuart to fight his own battle in court and we'll call it quits.'

'Stuart covered for us. I can't do that.' He clenches his hands but he looks little next to Ralph. 'Listen to yourself, man.'

'NO!' Ralph punches the wall behind the tramp's head. 'YOU listen to me, William Chimes. You listen REALLY CAREFULLY! You need to save your own skin, not Stu Baxter's.'

The tramp's mouth drops open. His eyes are wide. When he speaks it's so quiet I have to listen really close.

'Ralph Jackson, are you telling me you set Stuart up? You led the police to him?'

Ralph's eyes sparkle and his mouth twists again. 'No one can prove anything, William. I'm cleverer than the lot of you. As far as you're concerned, I just stood in the woods and watched them arrest him.'

He leans so close to the tramp that their noses are nearly touching. Ralph's hooky big nose. The tramp's squishy purple one.

'But you, Bill my old chum,' Ralph prods the tramp hard in the chest so that the tramp coughs, 'haven't covered your arse so well, so KEEP QUIET,' he prods him again—cough— 'OR,' prod—cough-cough-cough, 'I'M PAYING THE POLICE A VISIT.'

Ralph thumps the tramp in the gut so he bends over, mouth opening and closing like a dying fish.

I step back. The garage and the tramp and Ralph whizz around and around me. I grab Timmer's collar. The Backwards is fading. We've got to get away from here, Timmer. I want to leave now!

I start to run to the fields, away away away from the garage and the burnings and the bad bad bad stuff. My scar hurts. My eyes sting. It wasn't the tramp, it was Ralph. *Ralph* is a bad 'un. *He* called the police to catch Dad so he would go to prison. *He* wouldn't let the tramp save Dad from prison. He's bad. He's bad. He's not my mate.

I'm not doing the bloody burning. I'm bloody not!

Chapter Twenty-Six

Timmer and me get to the river. Behind my eyes
aches. Everything isn't what you think it is—Dad
isn't in prison, the tramp isn't just the tramp, Ralph isn't a
good 'un, everyone knows everyone and it's all a tangled
mess. It's dark and still here but I'm not tricked: everything is waiting. Now, the tramp's terrible Backwards will
come.

Timmer sticks to me like glue. There's a low growl in
his throat all the time and his hackles are up. Stay close,
stay close. We're going to finish this together, you and me.
We're going to see this story to the end, if we can stand
it—the proper end to the story—the real story without lies
in it. The story with all the frost in it.

The grass is dry because it's been so hot. The river is
deep and silent, all black and shimmery in the dark. It's

full of secrets, the river. I know it is. But they are hidden, down there with the fish and the stones and the rocks.

The Backwards is coming up behind me. I let it out near the garage land and now I can't stop it. They all twizzle round and round me—the river the fish the stones—faster and faster and faster so that my head spins and my eyes ache.

STOP!

The world stops spinning. **The Backwards night is here. I can see moonlight on the water. The river-moon is bright and wavy and beautiful. The leaves whisper on the trees. Someone is coming.** Turn round, Mikey, turn round.

The two figures come up the path from town. There's a little one in a hat and a tall one. I see the shape of them when they walk across the field. The little one isn't walking straight. He goes from one side to the other with an upsy-downsy walk. He's waving something in his hand. I think it's a bottle. The tall one is shouting. I can't hear what he's saying but he's waving his arms in the air. The little one in the hat moves away from him and starts running.

Timmer leans against me. A big heavy black lump sinks from my stomach down my legs and into my feet. It will make me stay here. I don't try to run.

I can't see them now because they are walking in front of the trees. My fingers have gone cold and I push them deep into Timmer's fur. I lift one foot up and wriggle my toes. There's frost on the ground. It crunches when I put my foot back down. **The tramp is singing out at the top of his voice. 'Don't tell!! Shhhhhhhhhhhhhhh!!'** I wrap my arms around me tight tight tight. The black is so thick that everything is dead—even the shadows. The cold bites hard because tonight it has teeth.

'Just can't keep your big mouth shut, can you?' the tall one shouts. His voice has a knife in it.

I hold my breath. Be careful, little fat one. Be careful.

They are up to the riverbank now. The little one in the hat stumbles a bit and sticks his arms out to stop falling.

'The fiiiiire . . . ' He shakes his head. 'Mustn't tell!!'

The tall one snarls and swipes out at him.

The little fat one moves quick, then ducks, and starts to run. The tall one kicks out to trip him up but misses again. The tall one slips. The fat one goes faster but he's all over the place. He has jerky legs.

I hug my knees close. My eyes are frozen open.

The little fat one is closer now. His hat is wonky. I see the tramp's face. His eyes are wide and frightened but they are sleep-walking eyes like he's not really here. He puffs as he runs past, his upsy-downsy run. I see his Backwards behind him: a big balloon holding him back and stopping him running too fast.

Here comes the tall one, fast now. The tramp drops his bottle and keeps going. Ralph's eyes glitter and the tight muscle on his face twitches because he is clenching his teeth together so hard. The naked curvy woman smiles as she goes by.

I don't turn to watch them by the riverbank. I stare straight ahead into the field.

The river is behind me. The moon shines down. I hear the thumps. The tramp cries out.

I look up into the night sky—it is full of stars.

Something cracks. Someone yells.

My ears are under water and it's all far away. Timmer whines. I hold my hand on his head. He goes quiet.

It's silent now except for Ralph's heavy breathing. I don't move. **I hear him splashing his hands in the river. His knees crack as he stands up.** The moon is shining on Timmer's head. It looks like he has a white bit on his head but he hasn't. **I can't see Ralph's face as he walks past me. He is looking down at the grass, hanging his head.**

I don't want to look at Ralph any more.

I turn downstream towards the bridge.

The tramp is lying at the side of the river. His Backwards has burst and it's spreading out in a big pool all around him.

I walk to him and kneel down in the grass.

His hands are trying to touch his face but he can't move his arms. His eyes are scared. He shudders. I can see where the Backwards is coming out—there's a big black hole on the side of his head.

I reach out to put my hand on him, like I do to Timmer, but he can't feel me.

He shudders again.

He's scared, Timmer. He's so scared. I want to help but I don't know what to do.

His legs twitch and he pushes his head out the water. He looks around but he can't see me. He's crying, Timmer.

I dig my nails into my jeans.

He's crying.

There's a quiet bit in the dark. The tramp feels it too. He moves his head so he can see the other side of the riverbank. His face goes soft. His mouth has a tiny smile.

I look where he's looking.

A bittern is standing in the reeds, watching us.

It bows down low, puffing up round its neck. A booming noise rings out over the fields and up to the stars. The reeds and the trees stop for a moment to listen.

It's the special bittern-voice.

This must be the Dad-bittern.

He's singing for the tramp, that's what he's doing. He's singing for him.

I look back to the tramp. He's still, now.

Chapter Twenty-Seven

I don't move. The river goes by. The moon watches me. I get it—I've worked it all out. Ralph killed the tramp to stop him talking. Ralph got the police to catch Dad so he went to prison. Ralph tipped off the black-and-whites.

I pull the photo of Mum and Dad and me from my back pocket. Dad is smiling. He's got his arm round Little Mikey and Little Mikey is looking up at him. Mum's eyes are shining. We were all in a little circle together.

Something funny is happening to the shadows. The dark all over the fields is moving. The dark is turning into shadow-people. All across the fields, they are creeping towards me. Black with red burning eyes . . . a black army, all coming for me. I clench my fists. My eyes are stinging. Timmer growls. Closer they come. All around me. Shadow faces right up close. A circle of them, spreading out into the distance.

I clench my fists tight. I can't fight them. Not even with Timmer. I think about Meg at the river today. About what she said.

I take a deep breath. I turn round and look them in the face. Eye to eye. My belly is tight. 'What is it?' My voice cracks. 'What? WHAT?!'

'Ralph, Ralph, Ralph . . . ' they sing and stamp their feet, 'Ralph, Ralph, Ralph . . . ' They press in closer and closer. 'Ralph, Ralph, Ralph . . . '

I press my hands on my ears but they are waking up the shadows in my head. My shadows are singing too—right deep down, so I can't hear anything else.

'Ralph, Ralph, Ralph . . . '

The naked curvy woman. Dad's frightened face in the woods when the black-and-whites get him. The tramp lying in the river, eyes wide. All the dark is boiling up inside me. It's pushing at my eyes so that hot tears come out. It's pushing at my chest so that my heart is going mad. It's pushing down my legs so that I can't keep still.

'Ralph, Ralph, Ralph . . . '

I have to RUN . . .

The shadows cheer and open up to let me pass. They know where I'm going.

Timmer is at my side. He's strong and keeps right next to me. I can't feel my legs. A cloud crosses the moon.

Along the riverbank, towards the woods . . . I stumble in the dark because I can't see properly. I kick some branches out the way. Keep going, Mikey! Keep going!

'Hey! Is that you, Mikey?' Meg is standing in my way. She's all little in the dark. Her face is white. 'Did you hear it too? The bittern! I think the bittern was singing . . .'

I push past her. 'Ralph's a bad 'un!' I keep running. 'I'm going to get him!'

Meg grabs my arm, but I pull free.

'Don't go on your own, Mikey! Stop! It's not safe!'

Her voice goes far away because the shadows are getting louder. I won't stop. Through the bracken, into the trees, down the path . . . My feet drum on the ground. Round the corner and up to the row of three houses . . . The moonlight makes the roofs shine.

Ralph is standing at the gate, waiting.

I can't see his face but he's just leaning on the post, just *leaning* there. There's a voice in my head and it's snarling, like Timmer. My legs are tight. My fists are tight. My head is red red red.

'YOU KILLED THE TRAMP!'

My voice is a scream.

'YOU SET DAD UP!'

The shadows scream too. All of them. All the way up to the moon.

The muscle in Ralph's jaw goes twitchy. He straightens up. He doesn't say anything. He walks up the path to his house. He picks up a spanner as he goes past the paint pots by the door. He goes inside.

I'm shaking. The tramp's head was broken. All his Backwards came out. No more forwards. And Dad . . . and . . .

I can't keep still. The shadows have started a burning in my belly and it's so hot I want to shout and kick and scream. The flames inside hurt and it's all his fault. ALL HIS FAULT!

I run into the house after Ralph.

Where is he? He's a bad 'un.

'You're a BAD 'UN!'

Timmer's next to me. He barks. We run into the kitchen. Timmer first. Ralph's behind the door. He grabs Timmer by the neck. Timmer yelps.

'LET GO OF MY DOG!'

I run at him but Ralph hits him. Hard. Timmer cries. I stop. My face is wet. My belly is burning. I stand still. Timmer looks at me, his beautiful brown eyes. His tail is between his legs. *Help me, Mikey*, he's saying. My eyes sting.

'You're hurting him. LET HIM GO!'

I run at Ralph, but he's quick. He opens the pantry door and throws Timmer inside. He lands against the shelves and cries again. Ralph slams the door shut. He locks it and puts the key in his pocket. Timmer howls. I clench my teeth. My head hurts so much I can hardly see.

'Just you and me now, Mikey-boy.'

Ralph is quiet but it's not safe. I ache behind my eyes. He's going to see-saw. I feel the photo in my back pocket. It WAS Mum and Dad and me but it ISN'T Mum and Dad and me any more because of Ralph.

'You did it! You did all those things!!'

Ralph's lips twist and he steps forward. His eyes flash.

'Ah, but you *didn't*, Mikey, did you? You *didn't* do it?'

'Do what?'

Ralph's hand tightens on the spanner.

'We had a little arrangement, didn't we, mate? You were going to light a few matches for your old friend, Ralph. Not much to ask after all the *trouble*,' he hits the wall with his fist, 'I've taken with you.' Then soft. 'Now is it?'

He puts his head on one side. He comes closer. I can smell his breath. It's full of lies. Full of them. Timmer howls inside the cupboard.

He comes even closer. Long eyelashes. He strokes the side of my cheek with the spanner. Cold and smooth. He whispers to me.

'Do you know what happens to people who don't do as they promise, Mikey? Do you?'

The world is going swirly and cold. Not now. Please not now . . . I feel dizzy. I grab at the table so I don't fall over. Ralph smiles and steps away. I'm not strong enough to stop it. The Backwards is here.

Dave is standing by the other door. He looks smaller without the other lads. He's with the Backwards-Ralph.

'I'm sorry, Ralph. It just ain't right. You understand, don't yer?'

Backwards-Ralph smiles. His fists tighten.

'Oh, I understand all right.'

He thumps Dave in the belly.

I hold on to the table tight.

Dave cries out. Ralph steps back. His face is ugly.

'I understand that you agreed to help me out and you're letting me down last minute. That ain't right, Dave.' His fist comes down again. 'I was counting on you.'

Dave is on the floor. His voice is muffly.

'You can get someone else to do it for you, can't you? You don't need me . . . '

'Oh yes, I'm not stupid,' Ralph punches Dave again. His head knocks against the floor. Dave moans. 'I'm lining someone else up to help. Someone too stupid to work anything out . . . Think I need you?'

Ralph kicks him hard. Dave curls over.

I feel sick. I look at the floor. Everything is dark and quiet. I'm looking at Ralph's boots.

Mechanics' boots.

Just like Dad's.

The boots that kicked the tramp.

My eyes sting. My nose is snotty.

My head is black black black black black.

257

I can't get away from it. Timmer whines. I need my dog. I need him close. I grip the table hard.

The Backwards is going . . . The Now is coming back. **Dave is fading but I can hear him whisper up at Backwards-Ralph before he disappears.**

'Leave Mikey alone, Ralph. Just stay away from him . . . '

A balloon puffs up in my chest. Dave stood up for me. Ralph attacked him. Dave was being my mate. Ralph lied. I stand up. Timmer scratches on the door. I clench my fists.

Ralph is standing by the sink. The tap is dripping. His eyes are sparkly. His face is pink. He passes the spanner from one hand to the other. My head is so full of red it's going to burst.

'You're a bad 'un!'

Ralph smiles. 'Ah, but at least I'm not stupid, Mikey.'

There's a face looking in the window behind Ralph. Two faces. Three? I don't care. I don't care who it is.

'You killed the tramp! You hurt Dave!'

I take a step forward. I hate Ralph. I HATE HIM! The spanner rises high in the air.

'YOU SET DAD UP TO GO TO PRISON!'

I rush at him. I'm too slow. He dances away from me, quick. He laughs. He likes this. My head hurts and hurts.

'YES, Mikey slow-brain. And your dad was a slow-brain too.'

I run at him again. He darts away. The balloon is

getting bigger and bigger in me. I can see flames and shadows everywhere.

'And Bill as well. Do I need to spell it out for you? It was *my* plan and Bill screwed it up. A simple bloody insurance scam—could he do it? No! Think I put that plan together as an act of *charity*?' Spit is flying out his mouth. 'And could Bill keep his big mouth shut? No, he bloody couldn't. That would be too bloody easy, wouldn't it? Takes to the drink! Breaks down like a girl! Sings our crime to anyone who would listen! Soooooooooo . . . ' Ralph's face twists again. 'I had to shut his mouth for him . . . ' He steps forward. The spanner winks in the kitchen light. 'Just like I'm going to shut yours . . . '

The spanner comes down. The back door crashes open. Timmer barks. I duck. The spanner hits the sink. There's a black-and-white here—no, *two* black-and-whites. They grab at Ralph. They hold him tight. He spits at me. The veins in his forehead stick out.

'Ralph Jackson, we are arresting you for the murder of William Chimes . . . ' The black-and-white yells at him.

I fall back. Meg is next to me. She throws her arms around me. She's crying into my T-shirt.

'You're safe,' she sobs. 'You're safe.'

I sit on the floor. Ralph is struggling but he can't get away from them.

'You're DEAD, Mikey Baxter. DEAD! . . . '

'That's enough, son.' The black-and-whites pull him up the hallway outside. One of them is talking into a radio.

Timmer barks.

'The key in his pocket!' I'm on my feet. 'The key to get my dog out!'

The black-and-white throws it to me. My hands are shaking. Meg unlocks the door. Timmer is here! Timmer is licking my face—he's all right! He's all right. I put my face in his neck and hold him tight. My face is wet and I don't want Meg to see. She puts her hand on my shoulder.

'I was so worried about you.' Her voice is wobbly. 'I was going to get your mum after I saw you but then I saw a police car on the street. Ralph had tipped them off you were going to do an arson job on his house. He wanted you arrested. But you weren't there. You didn't do it! I got them to come here with me . . . ' She throws her arms round me and gives me a hug. 'And Ralph admitted to the murder in front of the police. He admitted it himself! And they heard him!'

I'm still holding Timmer tight when I look up. 'He was a bad 'un.'

Meg nods. 'He was. And he's going to prison with the other bad 'uns, Mikey.'

I put my hand on the bump of my scar. 'Do you think everyone in prison is a bad 'un, Meg?'

She starts to say something, then stops.

'Dad went to prison.' My voice is very small.

Meg bites her lip and rubs Timmer's ear. The tap is still dripping. The black-and-whites are talking outside in the garden but I can't hear what they're saying.

'Just because someone does something bad, it doesn't mean they are all bad, Mikey.' Meg's eyes are greener than green.

'Dad was a good 'un but he did something bad?'

Meg's face is smiley again. 'Yes, that's what I reckon.'

I wipe my face. I reach out and squeeze her arm to say thank you.

'I have to go.'

'Where to, Mikey?'

I pull at Timmer's collar. He's standing by Ralph's kitchen table. He cocks his leg up the side of it, then looks up at me and wags his tail.

'It's time I went back to see Dad.'

Chapter Twenty-Eight

I can't hear properly. The whole world is far away. The Backwards is everywhere. I can't get away from it. Clouds are blowing across the black sky but I can't feel the wind.

We walk home the back way across the fields, so I don't have to see the black-and-whites and Ralph. The cows are in the field near the river now. I clip the lead on Timmer as we walk through them. They watch me but they are not frightened. Old Mary has her calf close to her. I stop for a moment. The Backwards helped you, Old Mary. She stares with her brown quiet eyes. I look for Bess and her calf—they are over near the riverbank. The Backwards helped them too. And helped to catch Ralph, the bad 'un. Cackler said it would. But it hasn't finished yet. Not yet. The shadows are still wide awake. They pull at me.

Over the scrubland; rubbish piled up by the railings. I climb through the hole in our garden fence. I walk up our scruffy garden.

I know where I have to go but I'm scared. I'm scared. I'm scared. Timmer whines but he's a long way away. Sorry, Timmer-dog. You can't come here. You can't come with me.

The shed is black-full of shadows. It's watching me. It's waiting. It's licking its lips. It knows I have to come to it. I have to, to make this stop.

I walk up the path, around the apple tree, my hand reaches for the door. I push it open. Timmer hangs back. He sits under the tree. My eyes are crying and I can't stop them. I walk inside and stand still. The shadows are going mad in my ears. Screaming. Shouting.

'Hello, Mikey.'

The shed goes dead quiet. My ears pop. Dad is sitting on the suntan sunlounger chair. He is leaning back against the wall of the shed. He's wearing jeans and a stripy T-shirt. Dad is brighter than everything else: he's nearly shining. My throat puffs up.

'Hello, Dad,' I whisper.

He pats the suntan sunlounger chair—there's room for me too. 'Sit down, Mikey. Sit down, my son.'

My legs walk over to him and I sink down. He reaches over to touch my head. I flinch but I want him to all at the same time. He smiles a sad smile and he puts his hand down without touching me. I want to cry.

I look up. The frost has crept all over the ceiling of the shed. It twinkles like stars in the night sky. I have never seen it look so beautiful.

Dad raises his eyebrows and looks to the door. His neck is still sore.

It's starting. I push my feet hard against the floor and wait.

Backwards-Mum bursts in and slams the door against the wooden wall so the whole shed shakes. She's been crying but her face is bright red.

'You just couldn't help yourself, could you? Couldn't bloody help yourself.' Her voice is high and really really mad. She flings things out of her way—the green watering can, the plastic toolbox, a coil of rope—because she's looking for something. Her hands are shaking and she's not really watching what she's doing.

Backwards-Dad walks in behind her. He's got a red face too.

'I did it for all of us. The family.' There's a crack in his voice, like it's coming to bits.

Mum stands with her hands on her hips. 'Oh and how is arson—bloody ARSON—going to help? Hey? Hey?'

'Bill said he'd see me right! More money to help the family!'

Mum is jerking as she lifts her hand to brush hair out of her eyes. She pushes her lips together to stop them wobbling and her nostrils go wide. A tear runs down her cheek but she ignores it.

'And tell me, Oh-Great-One, how is a dad in prison going to help Mikey? Or me? You heard what the solicitor said about your chances at the trial next week. How many TIMES did I tell you to stay on the straight and narrow?'

Tears keep running down and down her cheeks like a silent waterfall but she doesn't take any notice.

Backwards-Dad makes this noise like he's being strangled and his fists clench really hard so that the knobbly bits are white.

I go still and make my fingers stiff.

He punches the wall of the shed HARD. There's a crack. It feels like someone smashes my head at the same time.

I flinch. Dad-next-to-me sucks through his teeth. He knows what is coming.

'I SAID,' Dad punches the wall again with each word, 'I SAID . . . Bill . . . Will . . . See . . . Us . . . Right . . . '

Blood is dripping off his hands.

Mum is shaking and holds on to the workbench to stop falling over.

'BUT HOW CAN HE?!' Her voice is so high and screamy it doesn't sound like Mum at all. 'You'll go to prison and WE WILL BE LEFT HERE ALL ALONE!'

All the edges of her are jaggedy like bits of broken glass. Even her voice is scratchy.

There is a huge empty hole opening up in my stomach and I'm going to fall down it. I grip on to the sunlounger but my hands slide off the plastic.

Dad's face twists up. His mouth looks like a snarly animal. He takes a step towards her. His fists are still clenched.

I hold my hands over my eyes but I open my fingers so that I can still see.

'It's not my fault!' his voice goes up to a scream. 'I did this for the FAMILY!'

Mum holds her hands over her eyes and crumples on the floor like scrunched up paper. Her face is all squashed and her mouth opens wide but no sound comes out. I can't bear it.

I stand up and start to walk over to her. Dad-next-to-me tries to catch my arm but he misses.

I can't bear this. I can't bear this. Everything is breaking. Everything is smashing up. It's so black around us that I can't see the shed any more.

Dad turns and punches the wall behind him.

Stop!—the two of you, please just . . .

'STOP!' Little Mikey is standing in the doorway. It's a winter's day, frosty outside. He's wearing a yellow woolly scarf.

I sag back down on the suntan-sunlounger. Winter frost. This happened on a frosty day.

He's pale and his bottom lip is wobbling.

'Stop,' he shouts. He stands a bit taller.

Dad turns round. Mum's tears start again. She shakes without making a sound.

'Quiet, Michael!' Dad moves towards him but Mum grabs his arm. He flicks her away as if she's a fly and she falls into the pile of plastic plant pots.

Little Mikey puts his hands on his ears and closes his eyes and starts to yell at the top of his voice.

'Stop! I'm sorry, I'm sorry, I'm sorry, I'm sorry just stop just stop just stop just stop I'm sorry I'm sorry I'm sorry I'm s . . . '

'QUIET!' Dad bellows. He raises his arms and he doesn't fit the shed any more. He's bigger than all the edges and the door.

'STUART!' Mum screams pushing herself up from the plant pots.

Dad spins round to look at her. His arms are flying but they move in slow motion. They are beautiful and brown and full of muscles. He knocks Little Mikey. Little Mikey's mouth is a round surprised hole. He falls sideways.

The sharp edge of the metal toolbox waits on the floor for Little Mikey's head. I can see its hungry teeth. They want to rip his head open. They want to eat him up.

My hands fly up to the back of my head. I scream.

Little Mikey is lying on the floor.

Mum crouches next to him.

Dad is pulling his own hair and his face is broken.

There is a hole down the back of Little Mikey's head. All the black in the shed is alive. The shadows, my shadows, are growing in it. Some of them scuttle into the corners. Some

267

of them whisper. Some of them disappear into Little Mikey and he still doesn't move.

The frost creeps in from the garden. Twinkles across the floor.

I swallow hard.

So this is it.

This is where it all began. The shadows. The frost. Everything.

I reach over to Little Mikey. I put my hand on his head and stroke his curly hair and make my fingers as soft as soft as soft. *His yellow scarf is going red.* I run my fingers over the bit in his cheek that turns into a dimple. My hands go shaky. I bite my lip. When the doctors wake you up, Little Mikey, you'll be me.

Dad bends down next to me. He tries to touch Little Mikey but Mum won't let him. She pushes him away—he just sags and lets her.

Mum picks up Little Mikey. He's all floppy like a dead rabbit.

The winter Backwards-sunlight shines in through the dirty window onto the pile of orange deckchairs and the barbecue and my blue Raleigh bike.

I sit back down on the suntan sunlounger.

Dad hasn't moved.

Mum looks down on him from the door. She's still clutching Little Mikey. Her top lip curls as if she can't stand him. Then she leaves.

Dad sits for a minute. He reaches out for where Little Mikey was lying. There is a dark puddle on the floor. His nostrils open wide and his eyes water. He jumps to his feet and runs out of the shed after Mum. He's staggering like he's drunk.

I don't move. The light is changing. I smell the grass-cuttings from the pile outside the shed. The grey light is coming in the window and lands on my leg. It's morning. The night is over. It's the Now.

Dad-next-to-me hasn't moved either. His cheeks are wet. His mouth moves but I can't hear what he's saying.

I lean a little closer.

Timmer patters into the shed from outside.

Dad-next-to-me is going see-through. I can see through him to the fishing nets on the wall of the shed. His mouth keeps moving but I still can't hear him. His face is lined and tired and under his eyes are bluey black. I move right next to him and put my face close to his. His eyes are sunshiney for a moment and then he speaks again.

'Sorry, my son,' he whispers. 'It was an accident.' He reaches out and his arm is nearly as clear as clingfilm. He puts his hand on my scar but I only feel a soft wind. He smiles and I ache.

'My boy. My Mikey.'

Chapter Twenty-Nine

I sit in the garden watching the sky. It's going to be hot again. Blackie starts the singing for the new day before all the other birds. Blackbirds are the first to sing in the morning and the last to sing at night: a blackbird-song-sandwich. He stands on the top of the fence between us and Albert. Timmer lifts his head from my leg and does a low woof. Blackie stays for a minute, then flies off. Timmer grunts and puts his head back on my leg. I stroke his back, curly rough fur. Me and my dog.

The shed door is wide open. There are no shadows in there any more. Dad is gone too. He said I was his boy. I swallow hard. I'm *still* his boy. Little Mikey was sparky and quick quick quick but I have my scar so I can see the Backwards.

Footsteps clatter down the path from the street. I sit up. Timmer's tail starts wagging.

'You nearly bloody scared me to death!' Mum runs round the corner of the house into the garden. She grabs me and hugs me hard, all squishy.

'MUM! You're home!' I squeeze her tight. I don't realize I am shaking till she hugs me. She's got littler since I last saw her.

'Where the hell have you been?' She pushes me away, kisses my forehead hard, and hugs me again. 'I got home last night as a surprise . . . you were bloody gone! I checked everywhere, couldn't find you. NO NOTE!' She shakes my shoulders. 'I phoned Cackler's farm because Pat said you might be there—Pat's at the farm now, I must call her—and they put me in touch with the police.' Her voice is starting to crack. She takes deep breaths, puts her hand on her chest. 'You worried me to death, Mikey.'

'I'm sorry,' I whisper.

Mum covers her face with her hands for a minute.

'The police told me all about it—the tramp, you at Ralph's house, the thing he did to Dad . . . then you run off into the dark . . .' She lets out a sob. 'God, what a night!'

'Ralph was a bad 'un.'

Mum brushes a bit of hair out of my face. 'What were you doing getting messed up with that man, love?'

I knit my fingers together. 'He said he would be my friend and take me to the beach. We had lunch together. And some drinks. And he showed me round the farm.'

Mum puts her arms round my shoulders and holds me tight.

'I thought he was a good 'un, but he wasn't.' I'm muffled because my head is on her shoulder.

'You should have told me . . . '

'You weren't here.'

Mum puts her hand under my chin and lifts my face so I look at her.

'I'm sorry I've not been around for you recently. I'm sorry. There's something I should have told you about Dad . . . ' Her voice starts to crack, but she keeps looking into my face. 'I didn't want to upset you because I'd always told you to stop thinking about him . . . I wanted to protect you . . . '

I sit very still. Mum strokes my hair and twists one of the curls round her finger. Blackie lands on the grass nearby. I reach out to him and he hops forwards for a few steps before he flies off again.

Mum smiles a sad smile. 'You're like your dad, the way you love nature.' She ruffles my hair. 'He found it so hard to adjust to prison life . . . '

'But he's not in prison any more, is he?' I whisper.

She takes a deep breath. 'Sort of, Mikey. He's still a prisoner but he had to go to hospital.'

'He's poorly?'

She puts her arm around me and kisses the top of my head. 'The prison called me in because Dad tried to . . . he tried to take his own . . . '

I think of the red mark round Dad's neck in the shed. I wrap my arms around me tight. Timmer sits right next to me, doesn't take his eyes off my face.

Mum sniffs and gurgles all at once and then whispers so softly I can hardly hear her. 'He is unconscious in hospital—that means he's asleep so you can't wake him up. The doctors don't know if . . . if . . . '

'Is he going to get better?' I whisper.

'I don't know, love.' Her voice is raggedy, breaking into little pieces. 'I don't know . . . '

The wind blows through the leaves of the apple tree. The sky is blue blue blue. Timmer looks up at me with his brown eyes. I rub behind his black ear. He puts his head on my knee. I need my dog.

Mum blows her nose. 'It's funny—they took your dad to hospital on the night that you thought you saw him in the shed . . . '

I close my eyes because they are hot and stinging. Dad wanted to talk to me that night. He wanted to talk to me very badly. He came to see me and I didn't want to listen.

I lean against her. We stay like that for ages. She's warm. She isn't far away any more. She's here properly with me, even though I know she's crying.

I put my hand in my jeans pocket. I pull out the photo. Mum and Dad and me on the beach. Smiling. Happy.

Mum strokes my face on the photo. Then she kisses

the top of my head. 'I think it's time we went there, again. Don't you, Mikey? Your special treat?'

I smile and I start to cry.

'Oh, sweetheart.' Her arms are a circle and I am safe.

'Can I bring someone with me, Mum?' My voice cracks.

Mum holds me away from her and raises her eyebrows. 'Who?'

'Meg. Cackler's granddaughter. She's my friend.'

Mum wipes the tears off my cheeks. 'Course she can come too.' She hugs me close. '*Course* she can.'

I stroke the soft silky bit on Timmer's ears. I wait as my head is settling like the silt going to the bottom of the river after it's been all stirred up.

I look out to the trees and the hills in the distance. Maybe they don't know if Dad will wake up, but I know something as clear as clear as clear. Dad came to see me when he was ill—even chased the Backwards-tramp away. He waited until I was ready to see him and he waited until it was all right. He stayed until I could understand.

Chapter Thirty

I am so happy that my face is aching from smiling. Mum and me and Timmer are on the bus and we're going to the beach. We've got the back seat. Top deck. We'll pick up Meg at the bus-stop in her village. Timmer is sitting at my feet. I don't think he likes it much but he'll be all right. Mum and me might go on the bus again soon but Timmer can't come with us that day, though. We might go and see Dad in hospital, even if he's still asleep. Mum says she'll see but it's not to worry about today. Today we're going to the beach.

She keeps looking at me and has this smile at the corner of her mouth. Her elbow is leaning on the seat in front and when she lifts her hand to brush the hair away from her face, she has this criss-cross pattern on her elbow.

The sun is smiling too. We are right in the countryside now. The land is flat and I can see for miles. Fields and fields of yellow and green. I wish I could fly today. I would stretch out my arms and go, go, go. I would fly around the bus and wave at Mum through the window to make her jump, and then I would race the bus to the sea. The fields would whizz beneath me.

This is like when I was little and we went on bus trips; my legs didn't reach the floor when I sat on the back seat. I used to bang my heels into the hard bit of the seat like a drum. We went on picnics when Dad . . . when he was still . . . before I needed Timmer.

I feel the seat swirl under me. The Backwards? Timmer licks my hand. Ha! Let the Backwards come. Last night mended the Backwards.

Little Mikey is sitting next to me. He's grinning like a monkey and he's got chocolate all round his mouth. He bashes his shoes into the bottom of the seat.

Boom ta ta, boom ta ta . . .

I copy him and tap my toes on the floor and then I start to do the air drums from the old Backwards' picnics. I had forgotten all about them, it was so long ago. We drum together—his little hands and my big ones.

Boom ta ta, boom ta ta . . .

Mum looks out the window.

Boom TA TA TA TAAAAAAAAAAAA.

Shiiiiiiiing. I hit the high hat cymbals. Shiiiing!!!!!

276

Mum blows her nose.

'You OK, Mum?'

'Play another game, love. Play another one. Maybe "I spy"? You start . . . '

So I look at Little Mikey and he winks at me. We look out the window for something to spy.

The bus stops. Meg gets on. She runs up the stairs and grins at me.

'Hello, Mikey and . . . ' she shrugs and laughs, 'Mikey's mum!'

'Hello, Meg!' Mum smiles. 'Call me Lisa. Come and join us!' She moves up. 'I understand I owe you a "thank you" for your help with my son last night.'

Meg squeezes in next to me. Her leg is squashed right next to mine.

'It was a bit scary. Gramps feels terrible that he didn't realize what was going on.'

'It wasn't his fault!' Mum says. 'He's the salt of the earth, your grandad. Nothing wrong with seeing the best in people . . . who would have thought . . . '

I shiver and look out the bus window. I can tell that Meg's watching me. She got the black-and-whites so Ralph didn't hurt me. I didn't think of that until now.

'Thank you for last night,' I whisper.

'You were a bit crazy,' she whispers back, 'but you were brave too.'

Timmer shuffles on the floor.

'It would all have gone wrong though, if it hadn't been for you.' Just for a second, I put my hand on hers.

Meg gives me the biggest smile in the world. Mum turns round. I look out the window so she can't see my face.

I feel as if I've swallowed a star.

The bus is going down the road next to the river now. It doesn't look like my river any more, it's really wide—the other side is miles away. There are boats—proper ones with sails, red, yellow, green—and seagulls bobbing on the water. I tap my feet on the bus floor. The air smells different too. Salty. The river's getting ready to go into the sea, just like Mr Oldfield said at school. Forwards forwards forwards.

I see the sea first. It starts as a little strip of white that nearly looks like the sky but not quite. Then you realize as you get closer that it's a different sort of blue and it's water. The best thing about the sea is that it goes on and on and on. No closed doors or walls—just quiet and water for as far as you can see.

The river is so wide now that the blue of the river blurs into the blue of the sea.

'Can you see that?' Meg leans against me, pointing out of the window. 'The little line of waves where the river water meets the sea?'

'Well spotted, Meg!' Mum smiles.

Chapter Thirty

So do I. Meg is good at noticing things.

Timmer pulls hard on the lead when we get off the bus. He hates cars and things because he is used to us walking everywhere. I can't remember when Mum and I last did things together like this. And Meg is here too. Mum and Meg and me and Timmer.

There are some shops with candy-floss and T-shirts and stuff next to the bus-stop—I walk past fast because the music and lights will muddle me. Mum says it doesn't matter, she'll come back later.

We go up the gravel path and then up the little sand dune to the tufty grass at the top.

Ahhhhhhhh, look at that, Timmer.

Look at that!

The beach is flat and still a bit wet and brilliant for running on and stretches so far you wouldn't ever have to stop. The wind sings in my ears just like I knew it would. I can hear the sea singing too. Timmer barks and pulls and wriggles in a circle so he wraps the lead round my legs. Mum laughs and her face is soft.

Shoes off, socks off, lead off—and Timmer and me and Meg are running running running . . . it's like we're nearly flying.

We're nearly bloody flying.

I could spend all day here. Timmer could too. He barks and leaps in the water and then out again and then runs in circles and then chases the seagulls and then he's back and barking and jumping through the waves. I meant to bring the tennis racket and ball so we could play fetch, but I forgot. It doesn't matter.

Meg jumps right in and splashes around but I stand just on the edge to start with so that the waves can only just reach my toes. They tickle them and then go back again. In and out. A big one is coming—you can tell by the rising bump in the sea and it crashes on the sand and reaches up to my feet. Cold and sparkly. So I go in further. I don't move for ages and the waves pull the sand onto my feet all the way to my ankles, like they are tucking them up in a sand bed.

This is where the river comes to, this sea. My river. The bittern's river. The tramp's river. She brings all the secrets with her and then washes them away.

I pull my feet free and crash into the next wave. Timmer yelps and crashes with me.

'Hey, look at this!' Meg is standing near a rock pool. Her jeans are folded up her legs.

I splash over to her. She lifts a lump of seaweed with a stick. I lean over. It's a crab, blacky-green with pincers. Timmer barks at it. It moves a bit but there's nowhere for it to go.

'Cool, hey?' Meg's eyes are shining. Her hair dances in the wind. Curls all over her face.

'It's a good 'un!'

Meg grins. She picks it up between her thumb and

finger and holds it across the biggest bit of the shell so it can't snap at her. Upside down, it's only got a little body.

'Gramps says that if a crab gets one of its legs broken off, it grows another one.'

'That's cool!'

'I know, I know . . . ' Meg puts it back in the rock pool and covers it with weed again. 'You could grow new arms . . . '

'Or legs . . . '

'Or head . . . ' Meg starts to giggle.

I like that. Things making themselves better. A lump comes into my throat. Maybe Dad will do that too.

Mum's waving at us from near the sand dunes. The wind sings to me as we walk up the beach. I love it. I want to stay here for ever.

'There's a chippie just down there, so I've bought us some fish'n'chips.' Mum hands round newspaper packages.

They smell sooooo good. Timmer sits right next to me with his best hungry-face. I start eating, salt'n'vinegar fizzes on my tongue. Timmer's dribbling, so I give him some too. He swallows them, all-in-one-gulp, then does his hungry-face again.

Mum's red hair is whipping around in the wind all over the place and she's laughing at us.

'Ahhh, this is the life.' She leans down on the sand and curls up on her side.

Meg is sitting back, elbows on the sand. 'Hey, Mikey, I was talking to Gramps about last night. He said—if it's all right with your mum—you'd be welcome to come and work a bit on the farm in your spare time.' Her toe rubs a curve in the sand. 'You know, now that Ralph has . . . has gone.'

Mum watches my face, eyebrows up.

There's the bestest feeling in the world bubbling up my throat.

'I can be with Old Mary and Bess . . . and the pigs . . . and the chickens and help with the milking and the feeding and moving the cows and EVERYTHING?'

Meg laughs.

I stand up and do my jig. Mum laughs too and Meg claps her hands. I run around and wiggle my bum and do my bendy-leg dance. Timmer barks and dances too.

'I take it that's a "yes" then!' Meg giggles. 'Gramps thinks you're brilliant with animals.' She turns to look at Mum.

Mum smiles. 'How could I say no after that little performance?'

I run over and give her a hug. She sort of leans into me. She's nearly as happy as I am. Mum smiles and shuts her eyes.

'You're still a softie, Mikey, underneath it all, aren't you, love?'

Underneath what? I don't know what she means but

her face looks so happy, I don't care. It means something good, I'm sure. Mum's breathing gets slower. I think she's nearly asleep.

Meg stands up. 'I'm going to see if there are any more crabs—coming?'

Mum gives a little snore. She looks better than she's been for ages.

'In a minute, Meg.'

'See you later, Cackler's boy!' She laughs and walks away.

The wind has gone quieter now; it's having a rest like Mum. I love the swishing of the waves. I close my eyes. The sea sings to the Backwards in my head. I feel the world go swirly around me. It's coming, Timmer, it's coming.

When I open my eyes, there's a blonde girl, nearly a woman, sitting just a little bit up from me. She's wearing a flowery skirt that's really short and her feet are buried in the sand. She's reading a magazine and the wind is blowing her hair in her face. It keeps blowing the pages too. She tucks her hair behind her ears and, as she lets go of it, the wind pulls the magazine up in the air. It flaps around like a paper bird. The woman stands up and laughs and chases it.

I see her face.

I grip Timmer's collar.

There's a man too. I hadn't noticed him. He's walking

along the beach towards us from the other direction. He's got black hair and he's wearing jeans and a black T-shirt. One of his hands is held over his eyes so he can see properly. The girl can't catch the magazine. She's running and stopping and missing it. He laughs. The wind whips the magazine in front of him and he jumps high to catch it.

I put my arms round Timmer's neck.

I have seen his face too.

He bows low and hands it over to the girl. She giggles and does a pretend curtsy.

'Thank you, kind sir,' says my Backwards mum.

'My pleasure, m'lady,' says my Backwards dad, 'Stuart at your service.'

I don't remember him looking like that. He has twinkly blue eyes. There are no bruises. No lines or scars.

He smiles and runs his hands through his hair. He's showing off to her, Timmer, that's what he's doing.

I pull my knees in close.

Mum looks at me but she can't see us, I can tell by her eyes.

She's beautiful, is Mum. Her face is all rosy and pretty. She doesn't tell him her name back. She rolls up the magazine and then shades her eyes from the sun.

Dad ruffles his hair again. He pulls out some cigarettes from the back pocket of his jeans and offers her one. Mum smiles at him and he drops the packet in the sand and his cheeks go a bit red.

He picks it up and holds out the packet again.

'Cigarette for the lady?'

Mum rubs one foot up the back of the other leg. Dad looks at her legs and Mum goes red too.

'I don't smoke.'

Dad grins. I had forgotten about that grin. He does it before he starts dancing or before he starts singing.

'Ah, go on, go on, m'lady. I'm a bad influence, me.'

Backwards-Mum takes one and her eyes are shining.

I hear some shuffling behind me. Mum in the Now is starting to stretch and yawn on her blanket. She does a waking-up sigh but her eyes are still closed. Timmer whines and I look back to the beach. Backwards-Mum-and-Dad are fading, fading, fading into nothing. All that is left is the wind and the sand and the sea.

Dad, he didn't look bad then did he? Did he, Timmer?

'I must have nodded off,' Mum says, eyes still closed.

'Mmmmm.'

'You all right, love?'

Mum is squinting with one eye closed and her hand held over her face as she looks up at me. She looks like the Backwards mum, but she's got more lines round her eyes.

'Yes.' I draw a circle in the sand, round and round and round. A question is building up inside and I can't keep it in. 'Did you meet Dad on this beach, Mum?'

She breathes in sharp, pulls herself up and hugs her

knees tight. She won't look at me but watches the waves in the distance. Meg is starting to walk back to us, getting bigger as she comes up the beach.

'Yes, love. Yes, love, I did.'

I can feel how sad Mum is from here.

'Why d'you ask? Did you remember me telling you?'

I shrug. It feels as if a scab has been pulled off something inside me and the skin under is really red and sore and I have to be careful.

Meg's here now. Her face is pink and shiny. 'Anyone fancy an ice-cream?'

'Yeah! Shall we, Mum?'

'Why not?' Mum laughs. 'Wouldn't be right to have a trip to the sea without one, would it now?'

I look from Meg to Mum to Timmer. We're at the beach, all together. I'm going to work on the farm. I've found my Forwards here on the beach. There is so much light in me, I could float away.

Mum and Meg walk back to the sand dunes. I walk behind them, scuffing my feet in the sand. I want the wind and the waves to sing in my ears for ever.

I look back and Timmer is standing really still, ears forward. He's watching something out at sea. I turn and look too.

Two figures, holding hands, are running along the sand and splashing in the waves.

Timmer wags his tail, staring at them. A cloud covers the sun, just for a moment. My belly goes tight. The man-figure looks as if he has curly blond hair. Not Dad's black hair—blond hair like me.

I squint to look harder. Timmer gives a low 'woof'. My heart is thumping extra-loud.

The wind blows and the cloud moves. The sun is bright again and I can't see them properly any more.

'Come on, slowcoach!' Mum calls from behind me. 'If you don't hurry the ice-cream man will go home!'

I stand for just a bit longer. The man figure is splashing the woman figure and she's laughing and running up the beach.

'Mikey! Hurry up!' Mum calls again.

I turn slowly and pick my way over the sand dunes towards the ice-cream van. I chew my lip to stop me from smiling. Timmer yaps at my heels and looks up at me as I walk.

It's no good, Timmer-dog. I pat his head. I don't know who it was—I couldn't see whether it was the Backwards-Dad or whether it was me when I am big.

The light of the sun on the water was too bright.

Acknowledgements

Many thanks to my wonderful year group and tutors on the MA in Writing for Young People at Bath Spa University for all of their support and inspiration in bringing Mikey and his story onto the page, and in particular to the course leader Julia Green. I am also indebted to Liz Cross, Jasmine Richards and the team at OUP and to my agent, Victoria Birkett, for their help and enthusiasm.

Thank you also to all those who helped me with my research including: Sandy Dunford and her many insights about children with learning difficulties; Jenni Mears at the City of Bristol College and her class of students who made me so welcome; Neil Darwent for his very useful tour around a Somerset dairy farm; Jim and Simon for their clarification of police matters; and the ever-helpful team at the RSPB who answered my endless questions about bitterns.

Most of all, thank you to my family and friends, especially to my parents, and to Jo, Neil, Simon, Angela and Shawn, for supporting me and encouraging me in the pursuit of my long-held dream to write for young people.

About the Author

SARAH HAMMOND was born and grew up in Lincolnshire. As a toddler, she wore out her copy of Beatrix Potter's *The Tale of Peter Rabbit* through enthusiastic overuse and she is just as passionate about books now as she was then.

For almost a decade, Sarah worked as a solicitor in the City. However, following a lifelong dream to write children's fiction, Sarah recently completed a masters degree in Writing for Young People at Bath Spa University.

The Night Sky in my Head is her debut novel.

Author's Note

I first met Mikey as I listened to a reading of a poem. Mikey was only a shadow at that time, but even though I couldn't quite make out his features and didn't know precisely who he was yet, I felt him very strongly. And I knew that I liked him a lot.

The poem was called 'Slow Reader' by Allan Ahlberg and it made my blood boil. It tells the story of a child who struggles in the slow readers' group while his siblings play in a football team or take part in the school play. I'd never really seen life through the eyes of someone who has learning challenges, and I was furious that he (because I imagined this child as a 'he') felt so inadequate.

As I walked back to my car after the reading, I decided there and then that I would write a story for this earnest and belittled shadow-boy, but I would give him a special talent, something no one else could do.

I took a peek at Mikey's life (by now he had a name) and saw him being taunted and jeered at. But his world was different: shadows whispered and frost sparkled extra-bright. As I watched, one of the taunts—about being 'backwards'—suspended mid-air and began to change its shape, taking on a completely different meaning . . .

I hope that you enjoyed reading Mikey's story. I'd love to hear what you think—you can get in touch with me via my website **www.sarahhammond.co.uk** if you want to drop me a line.

The Night Sky in my Head:

Questions for Readers

The Backwards

Some of the characters in *The Night Sky in my Head* doubt
Mikey's ability to see the Backwards. Do you think that
Mikey's 'gift' is real?

There were rumours that birds would not land in
Auschwitz, the notorious Nazi concentration camp, after the
Second World War. Many people are drawn to places where
wonderful miracles are reported to have happened, such as
Lourdes in France, to find their peace and to heal. Do you
think that places have memories—and that these memories
can be felt?

Mikey's Animals

Mikey finds his peace in the natural world and his best
friend in the whole world is his dog, Timmer. There are many
animals and birds that appear in the book—Timmer, the
bittern, the cows and the calves on the farm. Why do you
think Mikey feels so at home with them? What role do you
think that they play in the story?

The Scar

'Little Mikey was sparky and quick quick quick but I have my scar so I can see the Backwards.'

Mikey has seen the world in a different way ever since the accident. How do you feel about the differences between Little Mikey and Mikey? Do you think that Mikey's attitude to his scar changes over the course of the story? Do you think that the Backwards is any compensation for what has happened to him? If yes, how?

Good 'uns and bad 'uns

'"Just because someone does something bad, it doesn't mean they are all bad, Mikey."'

Mikey gets rather confused about good 'uns and bad 'uns. Do you think he gets it right by the end of the story? How does his perception of Dad, Ralph, and Bill change? How many of the characters do you think are 'good 'uns' who do something 'bad'?

The Forwards

'It's no good, Timmer-dog. I pat his head. I don't know who it was—I couldn't see whether it was the Backwards-dad or whether it was me when I am big.'

At the end of the story, Mikey sees two figures running along the beach. Is it the Backwards or is it the Forwards? Who do you think they are? What do you think the Forwards holds for the characters in the book?

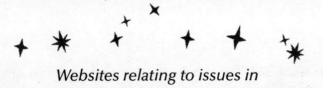

There are many organizations, such as the registered charity Pets As Therapy **(www.petsastherapy.org)**, who realize the importance of the therapeutic effect of spending time with animals. For example, there are schemes to take dogs and cats to hospitals, hospices, and care homes. Programmes such as Read 2 Dogs—when dogs are taken into schools—have been very successful. Children can lose their inhibitions and improve their literacy skills and confidence when reading to non-judgmental and supportive canine friends.

You can find more information about bitterns at **www.rspb.org.uk**. At the time of writing this note, the Royal Society for the Protection of Birds has 'red-listed' the bittern because of the global threat to the species, and the severe decline in its population in the UK.

The plight of the family and friends of prisoners has been described as the 'silent sentence'—it is not only the prisoner that suffers from the enforced separation from loved ones. Many organizations and schemes offer help and support in these circumstances. For instance, if Mikey's parents had become involved with the Storybook Dads programme, Dad could have recorded bedtime stories in prison for Mikey to replay and listen to before he went to sleep. Find out more at **www.storybookdads.org.uk**.

Here are a few of the many support groups and helplines that are available:

www.pffs.org.uk Prisoners' Families and Friends Service is described as an independent voluntary agency which has offered support for the relatives of prisoners for over four decades.

www.prisonersfamilieshelpline.org.uk Offenders' Families Helpline offers advice from the time of the prisoner's arrest to life beyond release from prison.

www.sharp-uk.org Support, help, and advice for relatives and friends of prisoners is given by SHARP which is free and confidential.